Mahjong Dreams from Nanjing to Taipei

Chinese-English Bilingual Edition

Roger R. Hale
Translated by Edgar Du

Four Jade Cultural & Creative Co. Ltd.

碰！麻將桌旁坐看百年中國

Mahjong Dreams from Nanjing to Taipei

Author : Roger R. Hale
作者：郝洛吉、錢德純
Translator : Edgar Du
譯者：Edgar Du
Editor : Tsai,Wun-Yu
編輯：蔡玟俞
Proofreader : Roger R. Hale、Tsai,Wun-Yu
校對：郝洛吉、錢德純、蔡玟俞
Art Designer : Chen,Wen-Yu
美術設計：陳玟諭

Publisher : Cheng,Hsien-Hao
發行人：程顯灝
Editor-in-Chief : Lu,Tzeng-Di
總編輯：呂增娣
Senior Editor : Wu,Ya-Fang
資深編輯：吳雅芳
Editor : Lan,Yun-Ting、Huang,Zih-Yu、
　　　　 Tsai,Wun-Yu
編輯：藍勻廷、黃子瑜、蔡玟俞
Art Director : Y-Tony
美術主編：劉錦堂
Art Editor : Chen,Wen-Yu、Lin,Yu-Ting
美術編輯：陳玟諭、林榆婷
Marketing Director : Lu,Tseng-Hui
行銷總監：呂增慧
Senior Marketing : Wu,Meng-Jeng
資深行銷：吳孟蓉
Marketing : Teng,Yee-Ling
行銷企劃：鄧愉霖

Publish by Four Jade Cultural & Creative Co. Ltd.
出版者：四塊玉文創有限公司
Address : 4F., No. 213, Sec. 2, Anhe Rd.,
　　　　　 Da'an Dist., Taipei City 106, Taiwan (R.O.C.)
地址：106 台北市大安區安和路 2 段 213 號 4 樓
Tel : 886-2-2377-4155
電話：(02) 2377-4155
Fax : 886-2-2377-4355
傳真：(02) 2377-4355
E-mail : service@sanyau.com.tw

General Distributor : DAI HO BOOK CO ., LTD.
總經銷：大和書報圖書股份有限公司

First Edition : 2021.03
初版：2021 年 03 月
Pricing : NTD 380
定價：新台幣 380 元
ISBN : 978-986-5510-54-1 (pbk.)
ISBN：978-986-5510-54-1（平裝）

國家圖書館出版品預行編目(CIP)資料

碰！麻將桌旁坐看百年中國 = Mahjong Dreams from Nanjing to Taipei / 郝洛吉, 錢德純作；Edgar Du 譯. -- 初版. -- 臺北市：四塊玉文創有限公司, 2021.03
　面；　公分
中英對照
ISBN 978-986-5510-54-1(平裝)

874.57　　　　　　　　110000474

SAN YAU
http://www.ju-zi.com.tw
三友圖書
友直 友諒 友多聞

Contents

Another Day: Taipei

"Johnny, this is the day I might die."

"I don't think so, Ma. I am quite sure this is not going to be your last day playing mahjong."

Lei Jun's son-in-law Johnny is probably right, of course; she won't die today. Lei Jun is nearly 103 years old and has lived through invasions by foreign powers, a civil war, two husbands and five childbirths. Her talk about death, as she looks into the mirror--right hand applying red lipstick while left hand straightens her hair--is simply a way to fortify herself against three formidable opponents at the mahjong table—friends who are all more than a decade younger than she. As she continues peering into the mirror, Lei Jun catches a glimpse of her pre-teen self.

"Johnny, I used to be quite a pretty girl, you know."

Lei Jun lives with her daughter, Angela, and her son-in-law Johnny, who works now as an investment specialist for a local bank. As she pretties herself in front of the mirror of this condominium in the heart of the most active shopping area in downtown Taipei City, Lei Jun continues to get mentally prepared for her mahjong game as if she were going to battle. She takes all in stride, her past and her future.

"Johnny, I've got a feeling I'm going to win today."

"Oh yea, Ma? I thought you said you're going to die today." Ignoring him, she continues slowly, not particularly caring whether he hears or responds to her questions.

"Yes, I'm feeling quite lucky for some reason. If I win, I'm going to take a day off tomorrow and treat the family to dinner with my winnings."

"How much do you think you are going to win?"

"You're teasing me Johnny; you know I can't predict that."

As she casually spars with Johnny, one of her favorite pastimes, Lei Jun continues to gaze into the mirror. Her youngest brother, 98-year-old Chaofeng, has just phoned a little while earlier and invited her for a visit after her mahjong game. Contact with Chaofeng always triggers memories of him as a child and of their other three siblings as well; the other three, her older sister, an older brother and a younger brother, have already passed away.

"Nanjing was a glorious city back then..."

"Did you say something to me? Do you need my assistance?"

"No, thank you, I am just talking to myself."

On this day in Taipei, her daughter Angela

is away from Taiwan visiting Johnny and Angela's daughter and son, who live in Canada. In addition, Jeanetta, their household helper, has requested a day off. Johnny had already decided to go into work late, after first accompanying his mother-in-law to her daily mahjong game.

"Johnny, isn't it correct that your maid has the day off today?"

"Ma, please don't call her 'my maid.' She is so good to you; may I remind you. She's been with us over 13 years and has done so much to raise your grandkids. She's an important part of our household."

"Johnny don't be so sensitive. I want to look through my keepsakes—just to make sure she hasn't stolen something."

"Ma, I told you I consider her to be part of our household, so I'd never suspect her of stealing anything. If you think she took some of your jewelry, you might as well blame me."

Lei Jun pauses for a long moment, as if she is considering such a possibility.

"Never mind. Never mind, Johnny. Of course, you didn't take anything; you're my daughter's husband. That would be impossible."

"OK, let me know if you need my help. I'll continue reading in the other room. However, please don't spend more than an hour. I've got to be at the bank for an important meeting by 11:00 am."

Johnny and Angela have discussed with Jeanetta many times about the fact that Lei Jun is prone to tease others around her, especially about stealing her belongings. Sometimes, her accusations are tongue-in-cheek; sometimes, Lei Jun is serious. Johnny has reminded Jeanetta this on multiple occasions:

"Jeanetta, when someone lives past 100 years of age, they're bound to have ideas and quirks that others around them simply cannot comprehend. We hope you overlook her accusations. We're not quite sure what she experienced when she was growing up that makes her prone to suspicion."

Jeanetta generally stays quiet and just smiles. She knows as well as they do how mischievous Lei Jun can be—how much she enjoys teasing those to whom she is closest; and she knows how Lei Jun occasionally becomes mistrustful of even those in her own family. Jeanetta, too, occasionally wonders whether someone has taken some of her own possessions, which she keeps hidden in the back of her desk drawer. In this way, Lei Jun and Jeanetta seem to understand each other well. Oftentimes, Jeannetta will playfully ask Lei Jun if she has seen anyone snooping in her room. Usually, this kind of exchange makes them both laugh together.

After Johnny is certain Lei Jun is finished conversing with him through the door, he walks back to his chair in the living room, where he begins to read the newspaper. In the privacy of her own room, with the door closed, Lei Jun continues looking into the mirror, past her own reflection to a different world, a time long since passed.

Earlier in Johnny's career he used to have a more high-powered and demanding job investing party assets on behalf the Kuomintang (KMT), requiring him to travel continuously around the world. During these last few years before retirement, he is taking it easy. He meets and exceeds his investment quota each month simply by maintaining his many friends in the industry whom he has cultivated for 40 years. Usually, Johnny goes into the office early, walks home for lunch and takes a long nap, then returns about 2:30 p.m. for another four hours before calling it a day.

Once Johnny returns to his reading chair and settles in again, he faintly hears Lei Jun say something else aloud; however, he remains seated this time, not sure she really wants him to respond.

"Johnny, are you sure you or your kids do not do drugs?"

A few minutes later, Johnny dutifully gets up and walks to Lei Jun's bedroom door.

"Ma, did you want me to answer your question? What nonsense about drugs are you talking about?"

Lei Jun continues to stare into the mirror behind her ablutions table in her bedroom. She pauses. Her hair has been primped; her makeup perfectly applied. She remains silent, forcing Johnny to just stand there, on one foot and then the other, for several minutes. Eventually, he turns around and walks back to his perch.

Johnny is a bit confused, slightly annoyed, but mostly humored by his mother-in-law. He knows her patterns well, and most of the time can anticipate all her jokes as well as her more serious monologues. He prides himself in staying ahead of her in every interaction, so that he can extract the most joy from each encounter. He and his wife are proud beyond words that Lei Jun is living such a long, vibrant life in their home.

This morning, Johnny senses Lei Jun is behaving slightly differently. She seems to be deviating from her usual habit of getting dressed, doing her ablutions and setting off to her mahjong game, making certain that she arrives at her friend's house a few minutes earlier than scheduled. Today, she is fixated on the past. It has been at least a month or two since she showed any interest in going through her keepsakes.

All Lei Jun's most cherished possessions she keeps in a leather-bound suitcase that looks like a small chest. Her mother gave her the suitcase when she left the house at age 15, and it, along with all the things she keeps inside, mean the world to her.

"Ma, are you ok? Do you want some help retrieving your suitcase?"

"Johnny, I'm fine; I don't need your help. I'm just thinking about my childhood. I don't think my friends will mind if I get there a little late today. I'm usually the first one to arrive...Opium is a terrible thing, you know...Johnny, you know what the hardest thing is about getting old...I keep trying to please people who are no longer here to care. My mom would be so proud of me if she were here.... She used to enjoy teasing me about everything."

By now, Johnny is not quite sure whether to respond or whether to ignore Lei Jun and her continuous, somewhat random monologue. The themes she touches on she has talked about before.

Lei Jun slumps down in her chair in front of the mirror. When reflective, as she is this morning, Johnny does not know whether to converse with her. He hesitates, then returns to his chair and yells back to Lei Jun from inside the living room.

"I am ready to walk you to your mahjong game whenever you want to go."

Lei Jun leans back down in her swivel chair anticipating the act of retrieving the keepsake suitcase which lies hidden beneath her bed. Like starting an internal motor, she softly hums a tune from the opera house where she used to train as a child.

Looking back over her shoulder into the mirror, she straightens and takes a deep breath, as if about to cliff dive from a precipice high above the water. Lei Jun lowers herself to the throw rug. Kneeling for a moment, Lei Jun then leans her head under the bed, extends her right arm and pulls out an 88-year-old leather-bound suitcase.

Johnny and Lei Jun often chat on two levels; in a comedic way that involves good-natured and witty teasing; and, on another more serious level on which each is deeply respectful of the other. Once more, Lei Jun calls to Johnny, and once more he gets up from his chair at the far end of the living room. He chuckles to himself quietly, then

Lei Jun speaks to him from inside her room, just loud enough for him to hear.

"Johnny, have I ever told you about why I left home at age 15?"

Johnny knows she is mostly talking to herself, that he need not respond at this point but he walks to her door as she begins going through her keepsakes, each carefully wrapped inside an item of clothing or cloth of some kind.

"Johnny, by the time I was nine or ten, life had begun to get complicated. I remember once being excited and happy about everything. The events in Nanjing and around China were about to change all that, forcing me look at the world in a new way."

Nanjing

Lei Jun was born in Nanjing during a gentle moment in 1917, between the Xinhai Revolution of 1911 that toppled the Qing Dynasty and the 1925 death of the founder of the Republic of China. She was the middle child with four siblings: older brother, older sister and two younger brothers. Of course, her parents had no idea that their newborn daughter would grow up to be passionate about mahjong or that her life would so perfectly mirror the triumph and tragedy over a century in modern-day China. Lei Jun's parents simply saw in her bright eyes that she might grow up to be a hardworking beauty, another set of hands around the house and store.

Both her mother and father came from relatively prosperous families near Nanjing and were introduced to each other by a friend who knew the families. Lei Jun's parents married in their early 20s and both were excited about raising a family and building a business together. They pooled money from their parents and a few well-to-do relatives and then purchased a building in a mostly commercial area near the main road, the backside of which would serve as their home while the front would be a small grocery store. It was in that building, on the main street near the center of the city, that Lei Jun lived her first 15 years.

Lei Jun's parents had been married in 1911, on the eve of the Xinhai Revolution that toppled the Qing Dynasty and promised a new era of the Republic of China. Lei Jun's father was a charismatic sort who promised his fiancée that he would soon be a rich man—that he was destined to build a profitable business.

"Everybody loves to be around me; how can we not be successful, you and I."

Lei Jun's mother was a hard-working, no-nonsense person who did not quite know how to understand her fiancée's bravado, but she loved his enthusiasm and his work ethic. Most of all, she liked how affectionate he was with her and how much he looked forward to bringing kids into the world.

Lei Jun's mother and father began building their business and having kids immediately after marriage. Lei Jun's older brother, Yongfeng, was born in 1912, which everyone told them was an auspicious year to be born in Nanjing. Yongfeng was lanky, and like Lei Jun, always taller than his peers while growing up. This same year was the start of the Republic of China, a government free from thousands of years of dynastic rule: No more eunuchs; foot binding or Manchu-style ponytails.

Three years after Yongfeng, Lei Jun's older

sister Lei Zhao was born, and a year and a half after her, Lei Jun herself came into the world. Lei Jun's father during these years continued bragging to his wife.

"You've given birth to a boy and two girls. We are blessed. Our son will surely look after his beautiful younger sisters."

While their first three children were infants and toddlers, Lei Jun's father and mother were building their business masterfully, slowly buying new products as the profits came in from existing stock items. Lei Jun's father worked 12 to 14 hours each day in the store, seven days a week, while his wife was generally busy on the other side of their building, in the house, taking care of the household and raising their first three young children.

Yongfeng was five years older than Lei Jun. From an early age he watched over the whole family and was revered by all. He sparred with his father, usually with tacit support from Lei Jun's mother. By age 13 or 14, Yongfeng had become a young leader of the family as well as the head of their family business. Lei Jun and Lei Zhao started approaching their brother instead of their father with questions about the store.

"We need to order more rice; we are starting to run low... How much should we charge for the small bowls that just got delivered?"

Lei Zhao was Lei Jun's best friend throughout their childhood years. Together, the two sisters had all the promise that two girls could hope for at that age: beauty; charm; energy; and a family with enough money to adequately fund their needs as they grew and flourished in Nanjing. They ran through the streets of their neighborhood interested in knowing everyone. Lei Zhao took great delight in leading her little sister.

"Come on sis, there is a new family who moved in down the street. Let's go see if there are any kids our own age."

During those early years, their father was planning to develop other franchises. For a while, their convenience store had indeed been making more money each year, as if the births of his first three children were somehow responsible for his good fortune. From dawn to dusk he stocked the shelves, manned the cash register, chatted with customers, shared tea with passing vendors, and occasionally went out at night with his biggest three or four suppliers. He would tell them all the same thing.

"We plan to open up a store in Yangzhou in a few years. My wife's family lives there and can assist us once we get our second store running."

In 1919, Lei Jun's first younger brother Huifeng was born and one calendar year after him, in 1920, the third boy and the baby of the family, Chaofeng. Whereas Huifeng was handsome, medium height and gregarious like Lei Jun, Chaofeng was quiet and unassuming, observing all the bigger people around him.

Lei Jun and Huifeng would spend hours together running up and down the aisles of their store engaging with customers.

"Hey there Mr.Li, where is Chuntao? We haven't seen her in a long time."

"She is at home, but I'll tell her you asked about her."

Huifeng was naturally handy, and later in life proved quite gifted in that area. As a child he always had a tool or a toy airplane in his hand, as if he himself were able to fly anywhere in the world by simply making a sound like an airplane engine.

"Zoom. Zoom. Watch out! Take cover."

As Huifeng zoomed down the aisles of their small store with a model airplane, Lei Jun stepped in front of him:

"Pilot Huifeng, where are you flying now?"

"Bombing the warlords...boom, boom!"

As an adult, Chaofeng grew to be tall like

the rest of his siblings, but his growth came late; during their childhood he was forever referred to as the shorter one. He was quiet, considerate and generally a supportive audience for his older siblings. He became trustworthy as the day is long. He and Lei Jun were quite close as young children, and their bond strengthened over the years at several key times throughout Lei Jun's life: once, after her divorce in Beijing in 1946 and then again more recently in Taipei City, after all the others in their immediate family had passed away.

Chaofeng eventually moved down the street from Lei Jun, in Taipei. The two siblings still see each other quite often, when Lei Jun is not consumed with the activities surrounding her mahjong games. At 98 years of age Chaofeng, too, has had an extraordinary life; but...this is a story about Lei Jun, a woman who soon turns 103 and still plays mahjong every day with three partners who are more than a decade younger than she.

All three of Lei Jun's brothers were talented in different ways. They stood united, protecting Lei Jun and Lei Zhao during the first 15 years of their sisters' lives. Yongfeng, tall and lanky, always with a goatee after age 14, was able to remain calm, even under pressure; Huifeng, usually with his hair cut short, was the handy one claiming that he could fix anything put before him; Chaofeng had a gentle reassuring voice and never lost track of the monetary value of things. He had spent his earliest days with his mother listening to her bargain with vendors. Later in life, people would joke that he was so good at keeping track of prices that he must carry an abacus on his back.

Regarding Lei Jun's physical development, her growth came early, and by nine years old she was taller and more mature than her peers. She was anxious about standing out, and Lei Jun remembers that about that same period in her life she was also anxious that her mother and older brother were suddenly having to spend more and more time managing the store—that her father was increasingly absent.

About that same time, the city of Nanjing was bustling with a great number of public ceremonies and celebrations, as well as an increasing number of mass disturbances. There was a rumor that Chiang Kaishek would become China's leader and that he would move the entire government to Nanjing. This in fact came to be a year or so later. When Lei Jun was 10 years old, Chiang settled in Nanjing along with his glamorous new wife, Soong Mayling and their large entourage of household servants. Lei Jun and Lei Zhao impersonated what they imagined Mayling might say to her new husband, for everyone had heard that she mostly spoke English.

In general, Lei Jun loved her studies, cherished her friends, was proud of every member of her household, and was full of enthusiasm about life. By the time she was ten years old she was active and engaged on many fronts: At school, Lei Jun was intelligent and popular; with her friends, she was beloved for her humor that always suggested a touch of irreverence; she was adored at home by her family.

At this same time, Lei Jun joined a youth group at the Nanjing Opera House that was a kilometer away from their house. She was quickly identified by the youth instructors as talented, and she responded to their encouragement by making the opera house a refuge from her house, the store, and school. Every day until her early teen years, Lei Jun would leave school, work at least a couple of hours in the store, and then join her friends at the opera house in the late afternoon and evening.

In the store, she and Lei Zhao stocked the shelves with large containers of noodles, rice, and beans. After a couple of hours, she would ask permission of her older brother to go to the opera house.

"Just finish putting those on the shelf, Lei Jun. Also, Mom needs you and your sister to keep an eye on your brothers, especially Chaofeng. She doesn't want him leaving the area around our house. Watch over him for half an hour and then after that you can go to the opera house."

When Chiang Kaishek first proclaimed himself the new leader of the Republic of China in 1926, and first announced that Nanjing would replace Beijing as the capital of the Republic, small businesses around the city celebrated in anticipation of increased commercial activity. Lei Jun's father was invited by his vendor of paper products—a man the family knew well—to go out on the town to commemorate the event. Before that night, Lei Jun's father had not really taken a significant break from the store or left his family alone since he had opened it nearly 15 years earlier. He surprised them all by staying away from the house and business for two nights and three days.

Lei Jun and her mom were sitting at the kitchen table for breakfast when Lei Jun inquired about her father. Sullen, her mother changed the subject.

"Eat your breakfast, Dear, and then run off to school. Yongfeng and I need you to come home right away after you finish school today; there will be chores at the store before you go to the opera house."

Lei Jun's once hardworking and attentive father had begun smoking opium. From that night forward, everything began to change in Lei Jun's household. Her father withdrew more and more from his duties as father, husband and business owner, descending into an opium-filled world introduced to him by their vendor of paper supplies. Yongfeng, at age 15, had become the head of the household.

As Lei Jun's father's opium habit grew, so expanded the losses from their small store. His loyal clientele, whom he had cultivated for many years, began to return less frequently. He spent fewer hours each day working, and when he was in the store, he attempted to take money from the till. Lei Jun's mother and Yongfeng remained vigilant and were, on most occasions, successful in blocking him from the cash box. They were able to eke out enough money each month to feed and clothe the household.

"Lei Zhao, Lei Jun, I need you both to come back to the store immediately after school today. Your dad has gone missing for two days now; I don't know where he is or when he will come back. We can't manage unless each one of us works for a few more hours each day."

One day after school, while Lei Jun and her sister were restocking the shelves, they heard their mother lose her temper for the first time. The vendor of paper products had paid a visit to the store, hoping to get an order from Yongfeng for wrapping paper and rope. Lei Jun's mother interrupted him as he was approaching the counter, behind which Yongfeng was standing. Paying no attention to the three or four customers who were in the store at the time, she shrieked at the man.

"Get out of this store! Don't ever come back! "

Occasionally, Lei Jun's father would emerge from his world in the opium dens and act almost normal for a few days, even a week or two, before disappearing and surrendering, once again, to his vicious addiction. Lei Jun was aware of the collective effort to keep her father away from the cash box—that he was constantly seeking money to buy his drug. However, for the most part, her life continued to be full and exciting, and her mom remained so steadfast and loving that Lei Jun ignored that she had emotionally lost touch with her father.

Between ages 11 and 15, Lei Jun spent every free moment at the opera house. She had been recognized as a talented youth by her opera trainers since she began at age nine. Now, in addition to operatic skills, she was also discovering how to connect and communicate with clients and patrons of opera, many of whom were important Kuomintang officials who were passing through town. Lei Jun paid special attention to those clients who came not only to listen to opera and to drink tea, but also to play mahjong with others in the back rooms of the opera house. Lei Jun took note of how the mahjong players pursued their games with passion. Whether she was serving tea, entertaining with a song or two, enacting a scene with one of her friends, Lei Jun surreptitiously watched over the mahjong games. At home, she would often tell her sister about her discoveries at the opera house:

"One day I will learn to play this game. If I become good, I can even make money."

In some ways, Lei Jun's first 15 years at home were the sweetest of times. Oblivious to the tumult in the bigger society, she played on the streets, worked at the store with her siblings, and spent as much time as she could at the opera house. Overlaying those fine memories of childhood was the sharp pain she felt recalling her father's addiction to opium. She became paralyzed at her father's increasingly aggressive behavior toward her and other family members. Then suddenly at age 15, Lei Jun's childhood ended abruptly, and she was forced to look at life differently.

Somehow, her parents had misread the cues from the heavens: Nanjing's sudden rise to national prominence had not been a blessing, but rather a curse. Lei Jun understood the significance of Nanjing becoming the most important city in China.

Instead of bestowing upon her household buckets of gold and immense good fortune, the gods had been marking the start of troubled times.

Chiang Kaishek and Soong Mayling had chosen her city in which to live and that fact alone stood out in her memory of childhood. On Lei Jun's walks each day from their store to the opera house she wondered if she might get to meet Soong Mayling one day. She and her sister were increasingly aware that Nanjing had become the center of the Republic of China.

"Lei Zhao, come quickly. I hear Soong Mayling might be coming this way. Wouldn't that be great if she came in our store to buy something."

"Lei Jun don't be silly. She would never do that by herself. She has so many servants she doesn't need to do a thing."

Beneath the surface of the exciting and bustling city of Nanjing, Lei Jun's family was in crisis. They were being profoundly challenged by her father's addiction. There was turmoil during this glamorous decade outside the capital city of Nanjing, the headquarters of the Republic of China. Turmoil also defined the culture inside the family store, where Lei Jun's mother and older brother attempted to carry on, as if nothing had changed. In fact, the fabric of Lei Jun's idyllic family life was being torn apart due to her father's addiction. They could no longer rely upon him for anything. Outside, Chiang Kaishek and Soong Mayling projected an image to the world of a country united, once and for all, poised to develop in a modern and rational fashion. This, too, was an illusion, and to anyone listening carefully, the loud drumbeat of war could be heard in the distance.

Teenage Life

When Lei Jun was age 15 and her sister Lei Zhao was 16 the year was 1932, and the world should have been their oyster. Nanjing was once again thriving as the capital of China. Businesses around the city were increasingly profitable and Lei Jun's family-run store should have been making more and more money, as the number of passersby in the city grew larger every year. However, her family had begun to experience turmoil reflective of the volatility in the country at large.

Lei Jun knew her father had smoked small amounts of opium gifted to him by eager vendors seeking a space for their product on the shelves of his once vibrant convenient store. When she was much younger, and the small grocery business was thriving, her father limited his opium indulgence to occasional work-related gatherings. However, following that fateful night of celebration in 1926, when it was announced that Nanjing would become the future capital of the Republic of China, his smoking habits changed dramatically. Over the next few years, Lei Jun's father gradually smoked more, eventually often binging and then disappearing from his household for days.

One day, not long after her 15th birthday, Lei Jun and her sister were sitting together in the kitchen while their mother was standing over the sink starting to sob. Their father entered the kitchen in an agitated state. Their mother must have known what he was going to say; she must have heard it from him earlier. In a slow, slurred speech, Lei Jun's father spoke. Far from coming of age with a sense of calm and security, the way one might if the world were truly her "oyster,"

Lei Jun suddenly confronted a family crisis that required her immediate attention.

"Your brother...isn't letting me into my own cash box. I...need some money for my own purposes. I found out I can make some good income if you two girls agree to work for the madam down the street. I talked to her yesterday; I told her that you both would start work there in a couple of weeks."

This bombshell required more than a gradual transition. Lei Jun stared for a long moment at her sister and then at her mother; the two sisters then exited the kitchen together without saying a word. Even on his worst days, when he was most high on opium, her father had, before that morning, been intensely loyal and protective of his family. Her mother had never suspected that her husband would become so slavish to his addiction that he would be willing to sell his own daughters in order to palliate his need for more of the drug.

After Lei Jun and Lei Zhao heard that their father was planning to sell them into prostitution in order to pay for more opium, their mother and brothers mobilized behind the scene. By the end of the week, Lei Zhao had agreed to marry her lover, a tailor 10 years older than she. The tailor already had a thriving business, as well as another family in Guangzhou, so Lei Zhao would have to accept the role of second wife and move in with him without a proper wedding; nevertheless, the members of the young man's family were fond of Lei Zhao, so the transition would be a smooth one. She was content with that arrangement, especially when she considered the alternative.

In Lei Jun's case, the short-term solution to her dilemma was also obvious. During that same short time that her older sister moved out of her childhood home to become a second wife to a Cantonese tailor, Lei Jun visited the opera house several times with her mother and her mother's younger sister, inquiring about alternative living arrangements. Lei Jun's mother unwaveringly prepared her to move out of the house.

"I know it has always been your dream to live at the opera house. Now, you'll get to live your dream."

"Mom, my dream is to be invited to live at the opera house because of my operatic talent, not to have my mom negotiate on my behalf."

Lei Jun's mom smiled at her daughter, undeterred. Later that day she presented Lei Jun with a beautiful leather-bound suitcase gifted to them that year by their largest vendor. It was bigger than a normal suitcase—it might better be called a small chest—with two brass latches holding down the top part; each latch was controlled by brass buttons. The small chest was of unusual quality, covered with thin, tough leather that had been molded tightly around a frame, giving the rectangular shape structure.

"Lei Jun, if you take good care of this, it might last you a hundred years."

The Nanjing Opera House, where Lei Jun had been attending evening classes and activities since she was nine years old, was one kilometer walk from the family store. Each year the school invited a few of the most talented and committed students, once they turned 16 or 17, to move into the dormitory in order to train more intensively. Ever since she began her youth program, Lei Jun had dreamed of being invited to live there, which would prove to her family that she was considered an operatic talent.

Lei Jun's mom did not understand or acknowledge the significance of the formal invitation, but they brought Lei Jun with them to visit the directors. The two middle-aged ladies were determined to make sure, by any means, to secure a room for Lei Jun away from home. She reluctantly accompanied them, trying to explain that it was a breach of protocol to approach her mentors with such a request. The two ladies laughed, ignoring Lei Jun's protestations, as they continued their walk to the opera house.

"Come on, Dear, I need to get back to the store soon. Your aunt is nice enough to join us, so, hurry up. Why're you dragging your feet?"

Lei Jun had been more affected over the past year by her father's deteriorating condition than either her sister or mom. She could not quite believe that her father, whom she loved so much and who used to dote on her as a young child, could ever do what he was proposing to do. Over the past several years in moments of frustration, Lei Jun had lashed out at him for it had been a long time since he had paid attention to her wellbeing. She had lost her dad; the warm, generous, loving man she remembered as a young child had died.

Lei Jun's mom and sister had already normalized his behavior. There were many opium addicts in Nanjing at the time, so it was easy to overlook Lei Jun's father's behavior. Casual opium use in Nanjing during Lei Jun's teenage years was pervasive, and it was understood by many that the government was somehow profiting from, even depending on, its wide usage. It was rumored that jealous wives even gave their husband opium to control their womanizing. This was certainly not the case in Lei Jun's household. Her father had been a workhorse for the family and a devoted husband before his frequent disappearances into the world of opium dens. He and Lei Jun's mother had been a happy and prosperous couple until, suddenly, he somehow lost control of himself.

All armies throughout China during the late 1920's depended on the revenue from taxing the sale of opium. A century earlier, British traders from the East India Company had sailed to India where opium was produced, then transported the drug to China and traded it for quality tea.

  Chapter 3 · Teenage Life

Finally, they sailed back to England and sold the Chinese tea for a high price. By the early part of the twentieth century, opium was being produced domestically all over China. Even after the fall of the Manchus, most armies—KMT, Communists, as well as those of Militarists—were partially funded through profits on opium sales. Later, the Japanese Imperial Army would also fund its activities in part from the opium trade in China.

Lei Jun was leaving her childhood with heightened anxiety and insecurity. Her father's addiction to opium was personal, not a social disease born out of general chaos, governmental inducement, or social dysfunction. He must have been weak on that day when his friends introduced him to the drug. After 15 years of working around the clock in the store he decided to relax and let himself go a bit. After that, he lacked what it took to get control of his desire for more of the opium-induced high. Lei Jun could not recall exactly when he became helplessly addicted, but she knew it was soon after Chiang, Mayling and their entourage arrived in her city for the first time. Lei Jun was 10 years old at that time and remembered that day clearly when Mayling came to settle in Nanjing.

As Lei Jun walked with her mother and aunt to the opera house, her mother told her that her father was no longer the same man he used to be— that he had been spending more and more time obsessed with finding only the purest opium in Nanjing. When he got ahold of money to acquire the best opium, he might go on smoking for days without stopping.

"Your father is losing weight and always looks disheveled. You know he must feel terrible about himself, so when he is not euphorically high, he is terribly depressed about what he has done to us all. Remaining at home will bring you a lifetime of misery, Dear. You must go immediately."

Chapter 3 • Teenage Life

As it turned out, the head of the youth training program at the opera house, as well as the overseer of the dormitory, were both fond of Lei Jun. In addition, Lei Jun's mom and aunt were, of course, persuasive. So, she was immediately invited to live at the dormitory.

"Lei Jun is a strong student with a good personality. She is outgoing and gets along with everyone and she is easy to work with. She is still 15 years old, but almost 16. As long as you allow her to join us and if she is ready to begin a more rigorous routine of dance, acrobatics and poetry recitation, then she can move in right away."

When Lei Jun heard her instructors compliment her operatic and social skills in front of her mother and her aunt, she smiled broadly. Beyond the compliment, living in the dormitory would allow her to socialize with her friends more freely, without obligations at home or at the store. The youth director introduced them all to Su Ming, her new roommate, one year older than Lei Jun. The two girls already liked and admired each other, so the new living arrangement promised to be a good fit.

Secretly, Lei Jun realized she would now get a chance to learn more mahjong while living at the opera house. She had first been exposed to the game while attending evening classes. One time her teacher had asked her to retrieve his jacket, and she accidentally wandered into the main hall, usually off limits for young students. In the smoke-filled corner of the room, there was a square table around which four animated players were hunched over, laughing heartily. One of the players was a woman.

From that day forward, Lei Jun took every opportunity to ask others about the rules of the game; she was curious how that lone woman was having fun in a gallery full of men. On certain days when government officials from all over China visited Nanjing, there might be three or four mahjong tables setup. For eight or ten hours at a time, players would battle each other, always with numerous onlookers. After a year or two at the opera house, Lei Jun was often asked to pour tea for the various players or, to entertain them with songs or vignettes from various operas. While doing so, she was quietly learning rules and mahjong etiquette.

Lei Jun never got a chance to play mahjong at the opera house, but strangely it became her training ground. As often as she could, Lei Jun sneaked to the secondary rooms off the kitchen and behind the stage where several times each week a mahjong table was set up. The players would be concentrating on their tiles so as not to lose money. She was bewitched by the overall rhythm, discourse and culture surrounding the game.

Lei Jun noticed that in every game of mahjong, however informal, there was a ritualistic acknowledgement of higher forces at play—luck, god, or fate. Banter between players was an important part of discourse before the start of the game. By listening carefully to what the players said to each other, Lei Jun acquired important information about individuals, politics, and life skills. She learned that to win consistently, she would have to understand her opponents and to anticipate what might be their next move. She noticed players always ate good food served to them halfway through the session, as if they were soldiers indulging in a little rest and relaxation after a well fought battle. There seemed to be no limitations put on competent and sociable woman mahjong players and they could, just like the men at the table, win or lose a significant amount of money.

At the opera house, some of the mahjong players were opera stars, others were workers and simple townspeople. Still others were dignitaries passing through Nanjing at a time when Nanjing was the governmental and cultural capital of China. Lei Jun listened closely to the chatter between players as she was serving tea, taking note of the fast-moving political situation unfolding outside in the streets of Nanjing and beyond.

At home again for the last time, Lei Jun folded her clothes and buried her keepsakes in her suitcase, putting each item purposefully in a special place. Her aunt gave her a diamond ring as a departure gift, which she placed carefully inside a faded yellow blanket. She then placed the folded blanket in the bottom back corner of her suitcase, where it has remained for 88 years.

Lei Jun showed her mom and her aunt another gift that her father had given to her on her eighth birthday. He had told her it was from the Qing Dynasty and that he had saved it from the time when he was a child.

"I will remember father for what he once was, not what he has become."

Lei Jun put the coin in a heavy sock and placed the sock near the faded yellow blanket. When she was finished packing everything, Lei Jun said goodbye to her brothers, mother and to her aunt. The three women embraced and cried together, then her mother finally chuckled, reminding Lei Jun that they would only be living one kilometer away.

At the opera house in 1932, Lei Jun and Su Ming quickly became best friends and surrogate sisters. Lei Jun was forced to realize things about herself and the world that she might otherwise never have come to know. For example, she soon understood the nature of her beauty, and quickly

Chapter 3 • Teenage Life

came to know the power that her beauty wielded over men. She also began to understand, more than most young women her age, that China was in chaos, and that the rules of the game for individuals navigating life alone, as she now was doing, were suddenly more flexible and fluid than usual. Beneath the day-to-day sense of calm and routine, life had become a game of survival. Lei Jun's early mastery of how to maneuver amidst chaos would serve her well.

Just as there had been daily drama at home with her family, there was the same at the opera house. However, in the quiet of the dormitory room with her best friend Su Ming, Lei Jun no longer had to struggle with her family members to keep their business afloat. Instead, she worked hard each day to refine her craft and to glean as much information as she could about mahjong and about the world outside the opera house.

Keepsakes: Taipei

Lei Jun continues her ritual of culling through her keepsakes, holding each item until it unlocks her memory and transports her to her past. She yells to Johnny who is in his reading chair in the living room.

"Johnny, please come here; I need to tell you something...If you help me, I'll give you a special coin that I received at my first wedding."

"You don't have to pay me for helping you, Ma. I'm happy to do so. However, I'll be sitting in my chair until you really need me. I'm the only other one at home, so keep your door open...Remember, we must leave in about an hour."

Even in the safety of Johnny and Angela's condominium in Taipei, Lei Jun is the same person she was as a teenager in Nanjing: Vigilance is the way to survive another day. Life continues coming at her, and she responds to each situation the best she can, like moving tiles on the mahjong table. Lei Jun will pursue scuffles, big or small, as a matter of principle, but she has no time or interest in getting bogged down with long-term arguments or grievances—be they differences with her siblings or conversations with Johnny. Lei Jun has decided that her son-in-law's comment is not worth pursuing at this moment, so she concentrates on her keepsakes instead.

Inspecting her possessions is always bittersweet. Each time Lei Jun scrutinized her past, she comes away looking a bit disheveled, as if she just returned from a more difficult time and place. Lei Jun is compelled to remember, but each time she does so, it hurts. Impassive at first, then closing her eyes and smelling the object before slowly turning it over in her hands. A blanket, photograph, coin, ring—they all have the same effect. Every keepsake takes on value far beyond its intrinsic market price; each item takes her back to a specific time.

From his chair in the other room Johnny tries to dissuade Lei Jun from going any further in her ritual. It always appears to him that she loses her jocular personality and becomes a different person while going over her keepsakes; she is for a short time consumed by retrospection and it is difficult to pull her back to the present.

"Ma, I guarantee all your valuables are right where you left them last time; and I am certain they'll be in the same place tonight when you return. Why don't you look through your suitcase when you come home this evening?"

Ignoring him, she kneels on the throw rug placed beside her bed and admires her leather-bound suitcase: surprisingly strong and durable, even after so many years. Next, Lei Jun carefully presses two buttons that release brass latches keeping her chest intact. Lei Jun lifts the cover at the same time Johnny yells from the other room:

"Everything alright in there? Do you still want me to come to your room?"

"No. I'm just fine. Stay where you are."

Lei Jun reaches into the farthest corner of her suitcase. Beneath all the other things is a neatly folded faded yellow blanket. As a toddler she had dragged the blanket around with her, up and down the aisles of her family's store. Closing her eyes, she brings it to her face. She recalls her father coming up from behind, embracing her, picking her up and twirling her around in the air. Lei Jun can even hear commotion on the street outside their convenience store. She can smell the mixture of produce, dust and incense that marks her association with their store and with her childhood.

Lei Jun places the blanket on top of other things in the suitcase, unfolds it and retrieves a diamond ring from its center. The ring, from her mother's younger sister, was given to Lei Jun when she moved into the opera house at age 15. Holding it tightly, as if to bring back her aunt, Lei Jun closes her eyes. Tears well up, and she quickly dabs them away with the yellow blanket, embarrassed that someone might observe her emotion. She is alone in her room, but Lei Jun can still hear her aunt's voice.

"Lei Jun keep this ring somewhere safe. You can always cash it in for money, in case you run into danger. But don't let anyone know you have it...and don't pawn it unless you must. It should be worth quite a bit one day."

She refolds the ring into the blanket, just like before, reaches down and places the blanket once again in the far corner of the suitcase. Next, Lei Jun takes the stack of black and white photographs bundled together with cotton twine that rests on top of all her other possessions. Undoing the loose knot that keeps the bundle intact, Lei Jun sifts through the photos, pulling out two, in particular: One is of her childhood friend, Su Ming. She and Su Ming are standing together, arm-in-arm, in front of the opera house, the day that Lei Jun moved in with her. The other picture is of Lei Jun as a young mother, twelve years later in Shanghai, cradling her first-born daughter, Bizha, who looks to be several months old.

She holds the photographs up to her cheeks, smells them both and sighs. She carefully ties them up again, as before, and returns the bundle of photos to where they were inside the chest. Lei Jun calls out to Johnny, forcing her mind to focus on the present.

"By the way, Johnny, Angela will be home tomorrow evening. Right?"

"Ma, yes her flight gets in tomorrow evening.

If you want, you can come with me to pick her up."

Satisfied with the sound of Johnny's voice, she keeps speaking.

"I am finishing up soon. I'm going to be a bit late to my mahjong game so the ladies will have to wait for me today."

Johnny gets up from his chair and walks slowly over to Lei Jun's room to converse with her at a closer range. He is curious to know how close to being finished she really is. By seeing how many of her things are spread out around her room he will be better be able to determine how much more time she will require.

"We need to leave the house in about a half an hour...By the way, why do you wrap each of your jewelry pieces so carefully in a piece of clothing?"

"Johnny, I wrap things up to hide them. If a thief opens up my suitcase, he might be confused and scared away by seeing only clothing...

Anyway, you are not supposed to be watching me like this, Johnny."

Lei Jun freezes for a moment, holding tightly to her jade bracelet that remains wrapped in a black wool shawl given to her by her grandmother. The bracelet is from Mr. Liu, a man she met while at the opera center—a man with whom she agreed to join in Hankou. Unlike the diamond ring, the photographs of Su Ming and of her first child—all of which she held closely—Lei Jun holds the jade bracelet at a distance, away from her body, as if she wants to control its power over her. She looks at the bracelet for longer than it takes to determine its hue, then quickly wraps it again in the black shawl and returns it to her suitcase.

Next, Lei Jun reaches to another far corner of her suitcase and gently pulls out an embroidered red cardigan sweater. Wrapped inside is a wood-framed photo. Lei Jun takes the photo and places it to the side, then brings the sweater to her face and inhales. Memories of her first days in Taiwan: plane ride with the soldiers to Hsinchu, second wedding, births of her youngest three children. Lei Jun's face contorts, expressing both joy and pain, as if two emotions are in a battle.

She puts her sweater down on her lap and picks up another photograph, circa 1958. She is seated with her husband and three young children, two boy toddlers and a newborn baby girl on her lap. Her 41-year-old self is joyful, while her husband proudly stands beside his family. Next to that picture, also inside the frame, Lei Jun is shaking the hand of 60-year-old first lady, Soong Mayling: entitled, graceful, proud, and still glamorous. That year was memorable to Lei Jun, not only because of the birth of her last child Angela, Johnny's wife, but also because her husband was unusually tense starting in August, when China began six weeks of intensive bombing of Kinmen, an island between the mainland and

Taiwan itself. Lei Jun remembers feeling at the time that Taiwan may not be able to buffer her, after all, from the travails of war.

Johnny retreats back to his chair in the living room while being chided by his mother-in-law.

"Johnny, I promise I will be done soon. I'll call when I need you to help put my chest back under the bed."

With others he would take umbrage at being told this and that; Johnny is a proud 64-year-old man. However, nothing Lei Jun says affects him too much. When dealing with his mother-in-law, Johnny's skin is thick as that of a buffalo. He is amused and proud that she lives with them, so accepts almost anything she says. Lei Jun continues talking, mostly for her own ears.

"Johnny, it's good to see that everything is okay; that all my valuables seem to be here...my knees are not what they used to be... I am wondering, though, about the way my coins were wrapped in this blanket. It looks like somebody might have taken them out to have a look. The blanket is not folded exactly as I always fold it...Fortunately, nothing is missing. It is a good thing I keep them all in my suitcase under my bed; otherwise, I might be sorry right now."

Lei Jun spends the next 15 minutes on the throw rug next to her 88-year-old suitcase, carefully counting the 144 tiles in her most cherished possession: a mahjong set given to her by the KMT ladies in Shanghai. The same women who had assisted her in giving birth to her two children pooled their money together to give her this gift after Bizha was born—encouraging her to return to the game table.

"Come on, Ma. No need to talk nonsense. Nobody is going to steal your things. We really must get going."

"Will you help me push this back underneath my bed to the very back, so nobody will be able to see it? Be careful; you never know when things in this world will have had enough and just collapse."

"Sure, Ma, I'll do that for you, if you allow me to enter your room."

"Of course. Come in, come in."

Lei Jun sits in her swivel chair watching Johnny kneel on her throw rug. She feels compelled to entertain Johnny while he is helping her out.

"When I first arrived at the opera house with my mom and my aunt, my best friend Su Ming commented on that suitcase you are pushing under the bed. She told us all, "Wow, that is a fancy suitcase. I am honored to be rooming with a girl who is as glamorous as Soong Mayling."

The Bigger Picture

Lei Jun first heard Soong Mayling's name in December 1927, as a ten-year-old working with her father to organize bottles on a shelf in their store. A customer spoke to him.

"Hey boss, did you hear the news yet, that General Chiang will marry Soong Mayling and they both plan to live in Nanjing? Your store is going to get really busy if Nanjing becomes the capital city."

"Hmm. Lei Jun, did you hear that? Mr. Chen here says that General Chiang will bring his new wife to Nanjing. Maybe you will get to meet her one day."

Lei Jun's father's comment was prescient: Her

destiny was intertwined with and impelled by Soong Mayling, who was 20 years older than she. The two women walked on earth during a similar time and in shared spaces. Through the lens of historical hindsight, it appears that Mayling's leadership in national issues pushed the boundaries of Lei Jun's otherwise largely predetermined existence. Mayling, too, was tossed around unwittingly by bigger forces; both Mayling's and Lei Jun's lives were dramatically altered by social unrest and political chaos, and both women endured an exaggeratedly tumultuous period, first in China and then later in Taiwan. At several key moments throughout this era, Mayling did appear to be at the helm, helping shape the narrative of history, and influencing the life of smaller actors such as Lei Jun.

Soong Mayling's family circumstances and upbringing, followed by her subsequent marriage to and shared life with Chiang Kaishek, were unique and extraordinary. Mayling no doubt increased the political fortune of her husband, Chiang, who retained a hold on power more or less for 50 years; few leaders in world history can claim such a feat. Much of his political longevity resulted from his union with Mayling, who delighted, enraged, manipulated and educated foreign leaders, especially Americans, over the many years.

Mayling was born in a suburb of Shanghai in 1898, the fourth of six children. Her parents, Charlie Soong and Nee Guizhen, bestowed in Mayling and her siblings the unusual combination of erudition, piety, ambition, and love for their motherland. Charlie was unusually adventuresome, energetic, and enterprising. He was a newly born-again evangelical Methodist, whereas Nee Guizhen's Christianity was rooted in several generations of well-established religious scholars. Mayling's parents were both devout Christians.

Charlie came originally from the island of Hainan, and as a young teenager eagerly made his way to America, first to work for his uncle's small shop in Boston's Chinatown. Restless, he soon left his uncle and took various jobs on oceangoing vessels. On one such venture, Charlie met a man who convinced him to convert to Christianity and then helped him find a patron to pay for Charlie's education at two prestigious American universities, Duke and then Vanderbilt. In return, Charlie was asked only to go back to China and preach the gospel as a Methodist missionary.

Charlie Soong fulfilled his promise to his benefactor, but soon after arriving back in China and partaking in the ministry, he became frustrated with his low pay for long days of missionary work. He turned to business, eventually making a fortune by printing and selling bibles in Chinese—devising how to cut costs dramatically by sourcing local material and talent. Mayling and her siblings shared a similar combination of traits passed to them by their two parents: a shared discourse informed by Christian piety and a "can do" entrepreneurial spirit.

During the last years of the nineteenth century, in addition to being a preacher and a businessperson, Charlie Soong became a revolutionary of sorts, joining a group that wished to overthrow the Manchu rulers of the Qing Dynasty. At church in Shanghai in 1894, Charlie met Dr. Sun Yatsen, who was the visionary leader of this movement that eventually instigated the Xinhai Revolution of 1911. Dr. Sun and Charlie became close friends and allies in their shared Christian faith, common Hakka heritage, and revolutionary zeal. Charlie gave generous financial support to implement his friend's vision.

Chiang was ten years older than Mayling; he was born in Zhejiang Province in a small town of Xikou in 1887. His father died when he was eight years old, and thereafter he was raised by his mother in a prosperous community of salt

 Chapter 5 · The Bigger Picture

merchants. In spite of relative economic security, Chiang grew up rebellious, feeling that he and his mother were battling the world alone. His legendary temper can be traced back to his earliest days. At age 20, Chiang went to military school in Japan for four years, the last two years of which he served in the Japanese Imperial Army. Through his military associations in China and Japan he developed a strong sense of Chinese nationalism, which during that time period meant working to free the country from dynastic rule.

Chiang came to know the powerful Soong family as a result of his mentor and founder of the Republic of China, Dr. Sun Yatsen. Dr. Sun had married Mayling's older sister Chingling, and it was a result of this union that Chiang learned about Mayling, who had been educated in the United States from a young age through college.

Mayling graduated from Wellesley College at the age of 18, receiving high honors, and then returned to China in 1917, the same year that Lei Jun was born in Nanjing. In 1920, three years after Mayling returned to Shanghai, Chiang had expressed to Dr. Sun his interest in marrying her. His mentor diligently passed on Chiang's request to the Soong family, the members of which all firmly rebuffed him for multiple reasons: Chiang had been married twice, was still married at that time and was known to have other women lovers; he was a soldier, not a scholar; and, he was not a Christian. Mayling was also opposed to Chiang's proposal, initially.

Even though Chiang's first attempt at marrying Mayling failed in 1920, he stayed the course and continued his long, drawn-out courting ritual by periodically writing her letters over those years. Meanwhile, Chiang was becoming increasingly well-known because of his military career, which had the effect of winning over most of the Soong's, except Chingling, who remained his critic and

Chapter 5 · The Bigger Picture

political adversary her entire life. In early summer of 1926, Chiang visited the Soong family members in Hankou, seeking their collective support of his leadership.

Ailing, the oldest of three Soong sisters, had come to embrace the idea of her sister's marriage to Chiang. Ailing presented Chiang a proposal: If he would marry Mayling, Ailing would promise to secure political and financial support for his government. Ailing was certain that with support from their Soong-Kung group, they could also raise funds from the wealthy class in Shanghai in order to secure Chiang's political future. Chiang was aware that both T.V. Soong, Mayling's older brother, and H.H. Kung, Ailing's husband, would be strong assets to his government. Chiang took note of his conversation with Ailing and, in particular, the details of her proposal, but he would not be able to implement it for another year and a half.

Chiang was thrilled with Ailing's proposal, for he had been thinking about Mayling romantically for six years. However, their marriage would be, from the beginning, a political union; and the timing was not yet right. Mayling was charming and possessed all the attributes that he himself lacked: charisma, education, sophistication, worldliness, good looks, and religious piety. Mayling increasingly saw marriage to Chiang as an opportunity to maintain her status around her older siblings. Moreover, she might be in a position to affect change on a large scale. In spite of her strong independent spirit, intelligence, and accomplishments, Mayling was enticed by Chiang's stature as a powerful military leader.

Chiang continued his day-to-day struggle for power and did not follow up with the proposal until over a year later. In May 1927, Chiang wrote to Mayling once again requesting her hand in marriage. By this time, he had proved to be a tough and shrewd political leader, but he had also initiated a ruthless Purge against Communists within the KMT party, for which Mayling's sister Chingling had been shocked and appalled. Chiang was ultimately forced by the party leadership to step down from his position as head of the military in August 1927. He returned to his hometown in Zhejiang Province for several months to contemplate his future.

Alone at home, without the burden of his job, Chiang was able to focus on consummating his union with Mayling. He traced the footsteps of Mayling and her mother to Japan, and when face-to-face with the two of them, he formally proposed. Mayling and her mother accepted his proposal with the condition that he sever romantic ties with his various women, and that he eventually learns to embrace Christianity. Chiang agreed and political opportunism converged with romance, setting the stage for the most powerful marriage of a generation. He proceeded to send his then wife Jenny Chen on a boat to New York, denying that they had been married, and he began a lifetime study of Christianity.

Mayling and Chiang held their wedding in Shanghai on December 1, 1927, honoring both the local tradition as well as a Christian tradition. Soon afterward, they moved to Nanjing. Eleven-year-old Lei Jun had just set out from her home on the main street when she heard the commotion that turned out to be the procession with Generalissimo's new wife Mayling arriving to town in February 1928. Mayling had become famous among girls and young women for her distinctive dresses and for the fact that she could never be seen wearing the same clothes twice.

Lei Jun and her sister tried to get a glimpse of Mayling.

"Lei Zhao, come quick. Look at the procession of black cars coming this way. It is the first lady,

Soong Mayling."

"Wah, I hear she is beautiful!"

Mayling's mastery of the English language was obviously first-rate; however, upon her return home to Shanghai after graduation, Mayling first had had to confront her unfamiliarity with Chinese language and culture. Conversant in Shanghainese dialect since she was a young child, Mayling still did not know how to read or write Mandarin. She began studying Mandarin intensively for the next several years with an old-style teacher who swayed back and forth when he read poetry.

Immediately following the wedding, Chiang returned to his post as military commander-in-chief of the KMT upon which he reinitiated his yet-to-be-completed Northern Expedition—a military campaign aimed to unify the country under a single KMT flag. Chiang had followed Dr. Sun since 1914, originally denouncing Western Imperialism and believing in socialism. However, his earlier

1927 Purge marked an ideological turning point in the life of the KMT and separated him from most other followers of Dr. Sun. Embracing his own interpretation of his mentor's ideas, Chiang had turned away from socialism, particularly those ideas promoted by the Soviets, and had at the same time softened his attitude toward Western Imperialists. Chiang maintained that he was fulfilling Dr. Sun's mandate, most importantly, by suppressing his dissenters and uniting the country around one KMT flag.

From the start, Mayling accompanied Chiang, grabbing the opportunity to steer the direction of the Republic of China and to help shape China's political future. Mayling's family of origin, generally referred to as the Soong-Kung clan, was, with one exception, mostly supportive of Chiang and Mayling and their nationalist interpretation of Dr. Sun Yatsen's mandate. After Dr. Sun died in 1925, his young, widowed wife Chingling chose to denounce

Chiang's betrayal of her husband's vision—a betrayal that had started with his heavy-handed Purge. For the next 30 years, she supported the rising Communist Party, which meant, in addition, being implicitly critical of her beloved younger sister Mayling. In spite of their differences, the two sisters remained cordially communicative until 1946, at the start of full civil war between the Nationalists and Communists.

Yet, within the confines of the city of Nanjing in 1928, and for much of the next ten years considered the golden decade for the Republic of China, Mayling and Chiang's reputations were rising along with that of their political party. The voices of their critics were increasingly muted, if not stifled all together. The Glorious Decade for the Kuomintang was unfolding in Lei Jun's hometown of Nanjing.

On a day in April 1928, Lei Jun called for her sister, who was inside their convenience store. The troops of the KMT's National Revolutionary Army marched through the center of town on the start of their second attempted campaign known as the Northern Expedition. Lei Zhao rushed out with her two little brothers. Huifeng and Chaofeng marched alongside the soldiers for several blocks until the sisters called them back to the house.

"Sis, I wonder if we are going to get a glimpse of Soong Mayling. I hear she is going to join the troops all the way to Beijing."

"What do you think she will wear? She can't wear a chipao, can she?"

Lei Jun's birthplace and her home for her first 19 years, Nanjing, continued to be transformed starting that year. Within several years this sleepy old town became a thriving, exciting, international capital. Nanjing's Glorious Decade was inserted between two major events in modern Chinese history, one considered by nearly all a success—The Northern Expedition, which mostly unified the country—the later one, The Nanjing Massacre, an ignominious disaster at the brutal start of the Second Sino-Japanese war. Lei Jun and the members of her immediate family had all, miraculously, left the city center by the time Japanese forces entered Nanjing, destroying all that had been built up during the prior decade, and killing hundreds of thousands of innocent city dwellers.

Lei Jun and Lei Zhao stood watching wistfully as the first lady elegantly passed in front of their store in a slow-moving black automobile. There were few cars on the roads of Nanjing at the time, so the car itself was a symbol of great wealth and influence. Through its window, Lei Jun could see that Mayling was dressed in a distinctive chipao. It was beyond Lei Jun's imagination that she would one day know this famous woman, much less that she would dine with her each year along with her husband-to-be, Mayling's secretary and most trusted assistant during her years with the KMT in Taiwan.

"Lei Zhao, look. Look! She is so young and so distinguished. I hear that her Daddy is rich and that she speaks perfect English."

From their first day together, Chiang and Mayling's marriage was of intense interest to Lei Jun. Their marriage was intermittently filled with love, affection and care, but most noteworthy was that their union was politically brilliant, defying the most basic arithmetic equation that one plus one equals two. In their case, one plus one resulted in far more than two for each of them as individuals, and, in some respects, for the region that they led, whether in Mainland China or in Taiwan. Throughout their years together, their union came to symbolize the best and the worst of attributes: fierce loyalty to family and friends, which descended at times to egregious favoritism and corruption; commitment to public service that

Chapter 5 • The Bigger Picture

they often defined too narrowly, when having to confront and incorporate left-leaning patriots.

The couple exuded a complex mix of new and old values when they first arrived in Nanjing as newlyweds. Chiang represented traditionalism of a sort, appearing stern and unyielding, speaking with a heavy local Zhejiang accent, and often referencing archaic Confucian sayings. Mayling, at the same time, embodied modernity, moving easily with all kinds of people, especially foreigners, speaking English fluently and often lecturing citizens about how they should take better care of themselves in order to realize a brighter future. Chiang was tentative and a bit awkward in front of a crowd, while Mayling carried herself with supreme confidence in the way she walked, dressed, and interacted with residents of Nanjing. She often had a playful modesty that endeared her especially to foreigners who yearned for some special insight into what they saw as a mysterious

Chinese culture.

Of all the various military threats facing Chiang and his regime between 1927 and 1937, the greatest existential challenge was from the Japanese. Yet throughout the decade, until he was finally forced by his own general to change his viewpoint, Chiang chose to focus his resources on battling two domestic threats to his regime: Communists and Militarists. He forcefully argued that only by suppressing these two domestic groups, and thereby unifying the country behind a single KMT flag, might China be able to resist the formidable Japanese military.

Eleven-year-old Lei Jun experienced, alongside others in Nanjing, jubilation after the successful completion of the Northern Expedition. Chiang's National Revolutionary Army (NRA) had retaken Beijing in a successful second attempt at reining in several powerful independently governed militias. One such region extended in the west from Xian to Lanzhou; another was in the south from Guilin to Canton; a third key area was that surrounding Datong; and most significant was the Beiyang region including Beijing and Manchuria. Lei Jun and her siblings lit firecrackers in front of their store for hours, as others all around the city rejoiced for what they all hoped would be the beginning of peace and stability around the country.

For the most part, Mayling settled well into her new married life, separated from her family who were mostly in Shanghai. However, marriage was not without its challenges. She intermittently suffered periods of depression: one time after a miscarriage in 1929, and another time after her mother died in 1931. In addition to accompanying her husband on most matters of business, Mayling maintained a busy agenda of her own, visiting orphans, wounded war veterans and the families of dead soldiers.

Mayling was generally more concerned than Chiang about their image as leaders on the world stage. She helped him to control his steely militaristic persona and to refine their message for the international community. She guided him to take on more moderate views for the country. As a result, most people were willing to look beyond the brutality he had inflicted on fellow countrymen and women during the Purge just a few years earlier. Mayling was now Chiang's most important human asset: intelligent, cunning, compassionate, ambitious, opportunistic, and indefatigable.

Mayling's sister Chingling, on the other hand, could not forgive her brother-in-law for his unabated suppression of leftist supporters and intellectuals. She criticized Mayling for standing by his side and, at times, partaking in what she deemed as immoral political deeds. Chingling continued criticizing their politics throughout the 1930s and was critical of their marriage. With regard to Chiang's new interest in Christianity, she famously commented:

"If he is a Christian, then I am not."

Chingling's blistering comment aside, Chiang had a few undeniably likable attributes. He was above all else loyal to his family and mentor, Dr. Sun Yatsen. Chiang showed great restraint when responding to Chingling or to his son, Chingguo, who had publicly branded him and Mayling during these years as "fascist military dictators." Along with loyalty, Chiang was conscientious. True to his promise to Mayling's mother, he studied the bible almost daily and then formally became a Christian at a small baptism ceremony at the family's church in Shanghai after three years of self-study. In addition, Chiang was a devoted husband to Mayling for many years. He relied on her ideas, relished her family connections, and admired her winning style with others.

During these years, Lei Jun attended the

opera house almost daily, oblivious for the most part to political events outside. It was not until she moved into the dormitory at the age of 15, in 1932, that Lei Jun began to take notice of cultural and political events that were taking place outside her direct sphere of life. Once she moved away from home, Lei Jun began to develop a keen sense that political events evolving outside her dorm room might, in fact, have a profound effect on her survival. She paid close attention to the chatter around the mahjong table in the backroom of the opera house. The information casually thrown around was important not only for what it taught her about the game itself, it was also important for understanding what was happening outside on the streets of Nanjing and beyond.

The success of the Chiang's second attempted Northern Expedition set the stage for the next decade in Nanjing referred to as the Republican Era, or the Golden Decade. It was marvelous to witness the transformation of a small town into a thriving international capital city. Lei Jun did not fully understand the significance of those years, other than to associate them with her own coming of age when life was full of hope and promise.

New Circle

Lei Jun lived in the Nanjing Opera House dormitory for four years, between 1932 and 1936. For the first three of those four years she resided with her best friend, Su Ming, who was one year older than she. The two young women shared everything, from hairbrush to their most intimate secrets. During that period Lei Jun honed a sense of independence and self-determination, and she and Su Ming developed a warm sisterhood that was foundational for building friendships throughout the rest of her life. Each night the two young women would chat about the day. Lei Jun entered early adulthood carrying an unusual mixture of tenacity, humility, confidence and exuberance about life—a blend of qualities that allowed her to navigate her way in a nation that was at war on multiple fronts.

Lei Jun was 19 years old in 1936 at the time that Su Ming left the opera house, moving to Hankou to live with her lover, Mr. Zou, the KMT Party Secretary. When Su Ming departed from Nanjing, she promised Lei Jun she would remain in close touch. It would not be long, she promised, before they were together again.

"You know he has a wife and other women, Su Ming. Why're you agreeing to this?"

"He is a good and generous man, I believe. I've no doubt this is the best thing for me to do. I may be able to sing better than you do, but I'm not as strong in my convictions."

Mr. Zou provided Su Ming with her own living quarters, separate from the main house but still on the same compound. Most of the time, Mr. Zou resided with his wife and children in the main house, but he made sure that Su Ming had everything she needed. Su Ming was satisfied with this arrangement. She grew to care for Mr. Zou and his family. Most of all, she appreciated the freedom and independence that he provided for her. These were chaotic times, when matters of life or death hung over everyone, consciously or subconsciously. Under the circumstances, Su Ming remained realistic and relatively optimistic, understanding her new living situation was not bad, considering her alternatives.

Mr. Zou's compound was an odd throwback to an earlier pre-revolutionary time, before 1911, where multiple families lived all together, and when the family structure did not adhere to preference for monogamy. Some modernists within the KMT might have looked askance at Mr. Zou for having a mistress, but he was an exemplary KMT official in other ways, so all had learned to turn a blind eye to such things. There was so much dissention and conflict during this period, that making changes to traditional family structures was low on most people's priority list. In addition, Hankou was smaller and more conservative and less apt to take on modern ideas than was Nanjing.

From the day Su Ming arrived in Hankou, she began sending missives inviting Lei Jun to join her in her separate quarters. Su Ming's departure had been a wake-up call for Lei Jun, suggesting to her that she, too, needed to consider her eventual departure from the opera house.

Lei Jun, there is plenty of space for you to join me for however long you want to stay. There is even a small room for you. Mr. Zou knows it will make me happy if you live here for a while. He wants you to know that he is familiar with several fine young men who are seeking a wife.

Every week, during her four years living in the dorm room, Lei Jun would rendezvous with her mother, brothers, and occasionally her sister. They would meet somewhere in the open market at the edge of town—tea shop, lunch table, sweet shop. For an hour or two, Lei Jun would catch up on the events at the house and in the store. In turn, she would update them with her life at the dormitory, invariably making them all laugh by relating some antic involving Su Ming and herself.

"Su Ming and I performed the other night in front of a small private group of knowledgeable opera fans. Our performance went well, and we received a hearty applause. However, I wasn't quite sure how we were able to complete it because Su Ming accidentally stepped on the edge of my pants early during our performance. It almost caused me to trip. We spent the remainder of the play suppressing our laughter."

Lei Jun always asked about her father.

"What state is he in? Is he trying to give up his addiction?"

Lei Jun's father's opium use was spinning

out of his control during the exact years that KMT made efforts to raise more money in the opium trade in order to fund the Encirclement Campaigns—a series of five military attacks on enclaves called "Soviets" that harbored the growing number of Communists. More specifically, opium addiction was devastating families in and around Nanjing. Between 1930 and 1932, Lei Jun's father had transitioned from being a functional addict to being incapacitated by his opium use, as a result making the declaration that forced both daughters to leave their childhood home.

After Lei Jun asked about her father, her mother, in turn, always asked her the same questions.

"Are you getting enough to eat? How is life away from home? Are you making any new friends?"

On one such meeting, after living in the dormitory for three years, Lei Jun mentioned that she had met a nice man from Hankou, who came often to the opera house. After slowly getting acquainted over the past year, he had begun taking an interest in her, asking her questions about her family.

"He asked me about all of you, but he took a special interest in Huifeng and Chaofeng. I told him how Huifeng could fix any broken object; he responded by suggesting that Huifeng go to a special training school for airplane mechanics...and, when I told him that Huifeng had just turned 16 years old, Mr. Liu said that was the perfect age to begin his training. I gave him our address and he said he would make sure that the principal of that school would contact Huifeng soon...."

"Who is this man, dear? Can we trust him?"

"His name is Mr. Liu. He told me he is Provincial Attorney General and lives in Hankou...He also is interested in helping Chaofeng if he can. I told him Chaofeng is everybody's friend and very clever—that he can excel at anything. Again, Mr. Liu told me that he would take care of getting him admitted into a special high school a short distance outside of Nanjing."

Mr. Liu was a political star, 15 years older than Lei Jun, who came often to Nanjing on business. As Provincial Attorney General in the Hankou area, he was charged with synchronizing the two judicial systems used in Hankou and Nanjing. These two cities were about 550 kilometers apart and were both controlled by the KMT at that time; however, the two cities competed, and the two judiciaries were sometimes at odds with each other about the political direction of the country. Whereas Nanjing eventually became the capital of the Republic of China, Hankou had been the center for the left wing of the party. It was one of Mr. Liu's duties to make sure that Hankou's judiciary was in line with the practices established at the capital, Nanjing.

Over a three-year period, between 1932 and 1935, Mr. Liu spent more and more time with Lei Jun. She was bright, engaged and interested in everyone. After slowly getting to know each other, whenever he visited Nanjing, Lei Jun fell in love with Mr. Liu. He was a passionate, experienced man. He did not expect the flood of emotions that he had unleashed from this promising young woman, so he was extremely attentive, aiming to be as grand as possible. For the next six months, before Lei Jun agreed to join him in Hankou, Mr. Liu and Lei Jun had a wonderful time together. However, Mr. Liu never spoke about his wife at home, his children, work, or beliefs; therefore, Lei Jun assumed she was his one and only love, and that she would have a lifetime to learn more about him.

Mr. Liu realized that she had become restless at the opera house and so he urged her to come with him to Hankou at the end of the year. Over the six months prior to Lei Jun's move to Hankou, Mr. Liu assiduously helped launch the careers of both Lei Jun's younger brothers. Lei Jun's imagination raced ahead, leading her to believe she was leaving Nanjing to marry the Provincial Attorney General from Hankou. She fantasized that she would soon be living a stable life as the first wife to an important man.

One day in early November 1936, Lei Jun packed all her belongings in her leather-bound suitcase, which was almost as big as a chest, and moved out of her dorm room at the opera house. She wrote to Su Ming, informing her friend of her imminent arrival.

I will be moving to Hankou next week and will let you know all the exciting details when I see you in person. I will visit you once I get settled.

As Lei Jun left the opera house, a small crowd

of teachers, students and staff came to the front of the building to see her off. Her family, except for her father, were also in the back of the crowd waving her goodbye. She had informed her mother about her move to Hankou, but Lei Jun did not expect any family members to be present.

Mr. Liu had seen Lei Jun earlier in the week, and he told her that he would arrange a carriage. He instructed her to travel to Hankou on her own, accompanied by two of his house servants. The women were impressed by the capital city, by Lei Jun's height and beauty, and by the fact that she had trained at an opera house. Encouraged by their positive attitude, Lei Jun continued to imagine, throughout the eight-hour trip, that she would be celebrated at Mr. Liu's house upon her arrival.

By the time the carriage arrived at the gates of Mr. Liu's compound in the early evening, Lei Jun's hopes and expectations for a bright future were in a heightened state. However, what transpired during the next ten minutes was disappointment that remained with her for over 80 years. Lei Jun was received by Mr. Liu's wife into the household with gentle, faint kindness. However, the gap between Lei Jun's expectations and reality could only be filled by disillusionment.

"My husband just told me all about you and your family. Please come inside and have some tea, for you must be tired after the long journey. Your room will be in the back of the house. It's all ready for you."

Lei Jun was sick to her stomach—the same feeling she had had once before, five years earlier when her father came down the stairs high on opium. However, she remained stoic and kindly greeted Mr. Liu's wife, a regal looking woman 15 years her senior with beautiful skin and a perfectly round face.

In the quiet of her own room that night, when

everyone in the house was asleep, Lei Jun allowed herself to absorb what had just happened. She was devastated and buried her head in her pillow uncontrollably sobbing for most of the night. When she finally stopped crying, her mind raced ahead, planning for the next morning. She knew Su Ming's address. She would pack her suitcase and leave it by the door, and then depart from the house as unobtrusively as possible, informing them that she wished to meet her best friend, whom she had not seen for nearly a year.

Lei Jun would disclose her dashed expectations to Su Ming and Mr. Zou, and then request their assistance. She could not return to Mr. Liu's house, and did not wish to see Mr. Liu ever again; she had mistaken his cues. Mr. Zou, who knew Mr. Liu, could send his servant to retrieve her small chest and Lei Jun would have to stay in Su Ming's quarters until she could figure out her next step.

The following morning, Lei Jun carried out

her plan exactly as she had conceived it the night before. After eating a small breakfast, she informed the servant that she would be leaving the house to visit her good friend. Lei Jun then slipped out the front gate, walking a kilometer or so away from the compound, toward the area that looked like it might be downtown. She hailed a rickshaw driver and directed him to Mr. Zou's mansion.

From that point, everything continued to unfold as planned. By afternoon, Lei Jun was inhabiting the small room inside Su Ming's quarters. Lei Jun was accepted warmly into Su Ming's abode, as had been promised, and later that afternoon Lei Jun's leather-bound suitcase was delivered to her room and placed beneath her bed. Lei Jun assured Mr. Zou that she would not be staying too long, but he protested.

"Nonsense, Lei Jun. You're welcome for as long as you wish to stay. With you here, Su Ming will be happy. In the meantime, I know a few patriotic young men who are seeking a good wife. I'll introduce you to some of these men over the coming months."

Lei Jun and Su Ming settled in again as housemates and quickly caught up on all matters. They had more freedom and spare time than they had had together at the opera house, so Lei Jun was able to pursue the game of mahjong in earnest. She had asked enough questions while at the opera house to fully understand how to play the game. She then set out to teach Su Ming the basics of the game.

The two friends next discovered additional members of Mr. Zou's household, Mr. Zou's wife's younger sister and Mr. Zou's male cousin, both of whom lived on the compound full-time. These two were willing to join them at a continuous, never ending, mahjong game. Over the next six months, the four players got together almost daily, at least for a short while, before one had to leave the game in order to fulfill duties or commitments. Any one game might take them days to complete. This slow motion allowed Lei Jun to carefully consider all her moves, replaying each one again and again, memorizing the tiles and speculating about which tiles her opponent might be holding. It was in Hankou at age 20 that Lei Jun became a strong and passionate mahjong player, a survival skill that allowed her, during the next phase in her life, to quickly and easily make friends in new cities, and also to channel her stress away from her high pressure life.

Put in even broader terms, mahjong for Lei Jun, soon after her stint at the opera house, came to represent freedom: freedom from her disappointment with her father; from Mr. Liu's mixed signals; and from anxiety about her future. When Lei Jun was concentrating on her tiles and trying to analyze the moves of the other three players, she was in control over her life and her surroundings.

Mr. Zou was good to his word on all issues. Over the next six months, he invited several men to the house to meet Lei Jun, in hopes that one would become a suitable husband for her. Mr. Zou's wife would sit the young couple together in the main sitting room where they would be free to chat alone. One time, Lei Jun and the young suitor walked outside in the garden together for several hours. Still, nothing ever came of such meetings, until Mr. Zou invited Wang Dacheng in February 1937.

Mr. Zou had come to know that this young man was seeking a suitable wife and he knew that Wang had returned from Germany five years earlier. Mr. Zou discovered that this man she was going to meet spent most of his time in Nanjing, but that he worked for a bilingual publication that required frequent travel. After Lei Jun moved in with Su Ming, Zou began approaching Wang, urging him to visit his house and to be introduced to an accomplished woman looking to get married.

Wang liked Mr. Zou, trusted his intentions, and took him up on his offer. As soon as Wang met Lei Jun, he felt he had found a suitable mate--a strong woman whose independence might allow him to carry on his work without being questioned or challenged on a daily basis. Wang felt secure about his standing within his work group, and so he ignored the disparaging comments he had heard about marriage from his boss and his cohorts. As long as he did not violate his vow of secrecy to his workplace, even with his wife, he figured there would not be a problem.

Mr. Zou told Lei Jun,

"Wang Dacheng is one of China's prized young men. He was studying law in Germany, but he decided to come home several years ago after one year of law school. He speaks and writes fluent German and wants to go back to Germany one day to complete his law degree. He's been working as a writer and translator for a Chinese-German press based in Nanjing for five years. Now, he tells me he wants to build a family. I told Mr. Wang that you are a talented opera performer, that you have a good attitude toward work and that you were one of the most popular young women in our capital city of Nanjing. I also mentioned that recently you have become an avid mahjong player. He'll be able to appreciate your beauty without my need to embellish."

After the third time back to Mr. Zou's compound to meet Lei Jun, Wang and Lei Jun began to discuss marriage. From the moment she met him, she had a feeling Wang was her man: handsome, tall, confident, educated, soft spoken, five years older and interested in her ideas. Wang still showed a sophisticated European style in the way he dressed and carried himself. Lei Jun told him about her childhood in Nanjing, and about her training at the opera house. They both spoke about wanting to have children. He was attracted to her good looks and strong character and he could see that she was tough, independent, self-reliant, and that she was mostly devoid of pretenses associated with class—an attitude that might bring too much attention. Wang felt that Lei Jun would make the perfect wife.

Lei Jun tried a few times to understand what, exactly, he did each day. Each time she inquired, she got a similar response, and that did not leave her entirely satisfied. Nevertheless, Lei Jun had already made up her mind, so he might have answered her query in almost any way, and it still would not have changed her mind at that point. She was ready to be married and had found her man.

"What is your work, exactly?"

"When I returned from Germany, I began working for an obscure German newspaper in

Nanjing, writing articles and translating interesting German writing into Chinese. My mother lives in Beijing, and my sister resides in Shanghai, so I will likely go often to those two places as well. My boss expects me to do whatever he asks."

Lei Jun married Wang Dacheng in May 1937 in a small private ceremony on Mr. Zou's compound, attended by only Su Ming, Mr. Zou, Mr. Zou's wife and Lei Jun's two mahjong partners, Mr. Zou's sister-in-law and his distant cousin. The wedding was an understated, happy event, and for a few years, Lei Jun felt she had hit the jackpot.

She now lived, most of the time, in her own small house in Hankou and was encouraged by her husband to visit her family members during the first few months after their marriage. By the time the Japanese attacked Nanjing in December of that same year, known infamously as the Nanjing Massacre, her parents had moved to Yangzhou, her oldest brother Yongfeng had just resettled in

Chongqing and her two younger brothers were both in boarding schools outside of the center of Nanjing. Lei Jun could be certain that none of them were killed or injured in the attack.

During the first year of marriage, Wang spent many days away from Jun Lei, sometimes up to a week at a time. He always advised her to stay in the house as much as possible. Several months after their wedding, Wang was often agitated when he did arrive home. The Japanese first bombed Beijing, Tianjin, and Shanghai, and the whole country was on heightened alert. Lei Jun could not justify questioning her husband's whereabouts at a time of national emergency.

For the first ten months of 1938, Hankou had become the new temporary location of Chiang's KMT government. In the same way that Nanjing had been transformed before her eyes ten years earlier, Lei Jun once again experienced a short-lived renaissance in Hankou. This time, however, all wondered how long it might be before the Japanese chose to attack this new government headquarters which similarly rested on the banks of the Yangtse River.

Lei Jun adjusted to marriage amidst war better than most could, by playing mahjong continuously. In addition to her games, she looked forward to receiving weekly letters from her mother, who was safe with her relatives in Yangzhou.

Lei Jun, I am so happy to hear about your small private wedding ceremony. I'm sick that I couldn't be there for you; however, the times are dangerous. We were able to sell our building fairly quickly. And, I told your older brother to take the money and invest it in a theater in Chongqing, which he has been talking about for a long time. We will join your cousins in Yangzhou for a few years. All you kids are living elsewhere now, so I don't mind so much living away from Nanjing. Maybe I can get your dad to give up his love of opium in a new environment. I can't wait to meet your husband. We think of you always. Love and congratulations. Most of all, stay safe.

The best days for the Republic of China in Nanjing—1932 to 1936—converged with Lei Jun's four years at the opera house. Then, while consumed with her own personal affairs—leaving the opera house, traveling to Hankou, moving in with Su Ming, and marrying Wang Dacheng—China itself was reeling with new developments that changed the course of history. Specifically, Chiang was kidnapped in Xian in December of 1936, and as a result, he was forced to dramatically change the direction of his foreign policy. By the early part of 1937, Chiang was refocusing his entire military strategy by concentrating all efforts on opposing Japan, rather than attacking Communists and Militarist. In July 1937, Chiang formally declared war against Japan; subsequently, the Japanese

Imperial Army immediately ramped up its attacks on the Chinese east coast, decisively winning battles in Beijing, Tianjin, and Shanghai. The year 1937 ended horrifically for Chiang and for all of China when the Japanese decimated Lei Jun's hometown of Nanjing, first by air and then by the Imperial Japanese infantry.

Tea with Johnny: Taipei

"Ma, will you be ready to leave the house after I push your suitcase under your bed?"

"Yes, I guess so...although I'm still upset about Mr. Liu. What bothers me most is that he wasn't being open with me about his wife and the several women living on his compound."

"Hmm. Is this the Mr. Liu who helped get your first little brother Huifeng a place in the prestigious high school, which then trained him to be a mechanic and led to a job with the ROC air force?"

"Stop teasing me Johnny... I'll explain to you why I'm so upset... let's drink some tea before heading out to mahjong."

"OK. I'll get some tea for us, but we must leave in 15 minutes. I need to get to the office."

Johnny gets up from his kneeling position beside Lei Jun's bed and goes into the kitchen area. He takes two mugs on the shelf, picks out some tea leaves from the tin container on the top of the counter and sprinkles a few into each of the two cups. Next, he fills them both with nearly boiling water from the thermos that rests beside the tin of tea. As he prepares the tea, Johnny continues.

"Ma, let me guess what you're really disturbed about this morning. You're thinking about your father. How could he have let himself get addicted to opium, right? That's why you asked about our kids and drugs."

"Well, it doesn't make sense to me, because he had built such a strong family...how he could let himself go like that...But don't change the subject, what I am most upset about is Mr. Liu, not my father's opium problem."

Lei Jun takes her purse from her bed and walks to the kitchen. She sits down at the table, placing her purse in the empty chair beside her—fully prepared to leave the house whenever Johnny indicates that they must go. She and Johnny have been through these subjects before and she knows what he likes to talk about—the issues about which he is most interested.

"Is this the same Mr. Liu who also helped get your youngest brother Chaofeng into school to be a navy hand in the port of Shanghai? You know how much I like to hear about Mr. Liu. He's an interesting character. I kind of admire him: Provincial District Attorney, big house, kind and generous to those he encountered during a chaotic time."

"If you hadn't already proved yourself such a good husband to my daughter, I would tell her to watch out with you."

"OK, then, if you don't want me to show an interest in Mr. Liu, tell me about your first husband. When did you find out that he was an intelligence agent? I still can't believe that when you married him you had no idea what kind of work he did."

"He told me, and everyone else, he was a journalist working for a bilingual publication— German and Chinese. I knew exactly where that place was in Nanjing; I used to walk by there all the time, thinking about how perfect his job was."

Lei Jun looks toward the living room, eager for some tea as if it will inoculate her from some of her most difficult memories. Again, she glances to her purse, placed in the seat beside her.

"You like to tease me, Johnny. Still, it's easier to talk about these things with you than it is to bring them up with Angela or my other kids. I just need to talk about them every once in a while. So,

I should thank you for listening, even though you remind me of Mr. Liu sometimes. You are arrogant, as he was."

"I am honored, Ma, truly. He was a great man, from what you have told me. You and your family might not have gotten out of Nanjing at the right time, were it not for Mr. Liu. I'm quite sure he helped save your lives."

"I know all that, Johnny; I am the one who told you that in the first place. But that doesn't mean he was a great man. He deceived me…"

"Regarding your husband, I am glad you moved on and married Angela's father, for obvious reasons, and I'm sure that it wasn't easy being married to a guy like Wang Dacheng during wartime. Nevertheless, he was a patriot—coming back from Germany in order to assist the KMT intelligence service. I still can't believe he lived so many years without telling others what he really did—who he worked for."

Johnny places a teacup in front of Lei Jun, walks to the other end of the table, sits downs and wraps his hands around his own mug. Johnny and Lei Jun sit across from one another, digging in for what seems like a choreographed fight scene; each is serious about controlling the narrative. All three issues—her father's addiction to opium, her first love Mr. Liu, and her first marriage to a spy—are topics that Johnny has heard numerous times over the years.

Johnny has heard about these issues from Angela's siblings, who all take varying degrees of interest. Johnny is confident about what he knows—almost as if he is more knowledgeable about the topics than Lei Jun is herself. Johnny's bold attitude agitates her. Still, they continue to chat.

"I was a simple girl, Johnny. For the longest time I didn't feel that I was supposed to question what my husband did each day or where he was going. It wasn't until I became pregnant, and began making certain demands, that I felt it was justified to be nosy and a bit suspicious. Only then did I question why he wasn't telling me the whole truth about things. Once his boss, Dai Li, came to see our baby Bizha, then I was able to put everything together. Bizha was just a few months old. That's when I figured out what Dacheng was doing each day."

"Yes, Ma, that's a hard one. But he couldn't have told you; he was sworn to secrecy. From what I know, he might have been killed had he told you; he was just fulfilling his duty and his promise."

Lei Jun glances at her purse sitting on the chair beside her, as if to signal to Johnny that she is prepared to leave the house anytime now. He grins slightly with a genuine appreciation for her sharp wit. Now, it seems that Johnny is the one holding things up, continuing the conversation.

"How many years ago was it that Mr. Liu

failed to be open with you? 83? And, regarding your husband, didn't you divorce in 1946, more than 70 years ago?"

"I don't remember dates. It's been a long time, I guess, but it doesn't feel that long to me."

For Lei Jun, time is irrelevant. The events in her life since childhood are collapsible, organized not chronologically, but rather in terms of importance. Often, she assumes that people representing different periods of her life know each other. It seems to her that all her good friends and family members should recognize each other, as if her strong feelings alone should bind them together.

"You remember Su Ming, don't you Johnny? She is such a wonderful friend, as dear to me as is my sister, you know. She understands my frustrations better than anyone."

"I've never met Su Ming. She died shortly after you came to Taiwan, didn't she—around

1950? From what you have told me about her, I wish I'd known her. You two must've had a great time together."

Lei Jun is unsettled, and Johnny takes the conversation in a new direction avoiding all the topics that are most uncomfortable for her.

"OK, Ma, one thing I want to know. When did you develop your love for playing mahjong? "

"I learned when I was living at the opera house, but I never played until I moved in with Su Ming in Hankou. I was 19 years old."

"And you have been playing ever since."

"And I have been playing ever since. If I didn't have mahjong, I would have gone crazy during all those years of war, married to a man who refused to tell me what he was doing or where he was going each day."

In recent years, Johnny has sparred less with Lei Jun than he used to, fearing that something might happen to her if she were to get too agitated.

"Well, let me ask you this...would you say that Angela's father was a good man?"

"Oh yes, Johnny, I have no complaints about either of my husbands. My first husband should never have married or had kids. He never told me anything about when I could expect to see him. But he was a good man who cared for me and cared for our two kids as much as he was able. As for Angela's father, you knew him. He was a great man: quiet; intelligent; hardworking; loyal; and good to his family."

"OK, Ma. That is nice to hear. I have never heard you comment about Wang Dacheng so kindly...I suggest you turn your focus on your mahjong game."

Lei Jun has no more interest discussing her life on this fine morning. She is mostly satisfied with where their short conversation has landed.

"I am ready to go, Johnny. I have told you enough secrets for one day. I must get to my mahjong game, so that my friends will not think that I have died. The first 40 years of my life were tough ones. I have had a hard life."

With that, Lei Jun picks up her purse and walks to the bench near the front door. She sits down with authority and puts on her walking shoes. Her mind has shifted from her past life to the impending game.

"I think it's right to arrive a bit late once in a while. I've a feeling I might win today. If I win, I want to take the family out to dinner with my earnings."

The Life of a Spy

When Wang Dacheng arrived in Shanghai harbor in 1932, he was 25 years old and passionate about helping lift his country to higher world status. Wang had gone to Germany as a college student seven years earlier, excelled and then been admitted to law school in Berlin. In the lead up to the federal German elections of that year, Wang generally sympathized with the nationalistic fervor that resulted in the Nazi party winning 230 seats in Parliament, roughly a third of the total number. However, he realized that if the trend were to continue, he would likely be excluded from meaningful participation in German society, due to his Chinese heritage. Mostly, German Nationalism triggered in Wang his own sense of pride for his homeland.

Much to the dismay of his mother, who urged him to stay in Germany and complete law school, Wang took leave after one year, with full intention of returning to complete his degree a few years later. He boarded an ocean liner for Shanghai with no specific job in mind. However, he had been in touch over the past year with a Kuomintang official who urged him to come to Nanjing and join the government.

As soon as he had bought his ticket back to China, Wang sent a telegram to this same KMT contact with arrival details into Shanghai harbor. He wrote that he looked forward to talking to the KMT official upon his return. Wang did not contact his mother in Beijing or his sister in Shanghai about his homecoming; he figured, instead, it would be best to show up at their doors and explain to them face-to-face what he had decided to do.

Wang deboarded the passenger ship and was swept up with hope and idealism about China—about what his country might become. Once on firm ground, he was immediately approached by two recruiters, who had been in touch with the Kuomintang official with whom he had been corresponding. These men invited Wang to have a meal with them near the port and over the next few hours they told him about a newly established department within the KMT. This division of the government, they said, was top secret and the president and other leaders could use his expert insights about Germany and his knowledge of the German language.

The two liaisons from Dai Li's Special Services Department (SSD) outlined to Wang what he would need to use as his cover at all times: Wang would be required to tell everyone, including his family, that he worked for a small German/Chinese press in Nanjing, helping translate, write articles and communicate with press outlets in Germany. They told him, as well, that they would give him keys for a flat in town, walking distance from the publishing house. In fact, Wang would be assisting the KMT in translation of military manuals, interpreting German politics, and assisting any German advisors when they came to help Chiang's army.

"This new agency you are about to join is one of the most important in the government. However, you will not get the recognition you deserve because you will be working for them in total secrecy. The young men and women we want to join us are the most patriotic of all citizens— ones committed to building the nation at any cost. You will report to a charismatic leader, who is one of Generalissimo Chiang's closest confidants, often serving as his personal bodyguard."

The SSD was created in the early 1930's, at a time when Chiang and Mayling came to know that the Communists were slowly winning a war of hearts and minds outside a few important KMT-held cities. With their own propaganda programs, the couple set out to bolster the image of the KMT. Under the umbrella of what was commonly referred to as Blue Shirts Society, Chiang developed several agencies, two of which would continue playing an important part in Lei Jun's life.

One such initiative was called The New Life Movement, which was an effort to evangelize common people, blending American Protestant beliefs with fascist ideals cultivated in Italy and Germany at the time. Mayling took a special interest in promulgating the 90 or so rules governing daily life outline in The New Life Movement. This regimen amplified certain ideas she had absorbed during her school days in the United States, and it also replicated the evangelistic zeal of her father that she recalled from childhood. The other agency under the umbrella of the Blue Shirts

Society, which was created during this period and impacted Lei Jun's life was the SSD. Unbeknownst to her throughout most of her marriage, the SSD organization employed her husband, Wang Dacheng.

At the end of their session with Wang, the recruiters formalized their agreement by giving him keys to a flat in Nanjing near the publishing house. There would be no written contract, they said, because that would expose them if such paperwork ever fell into the wrong hands. They told him that his new boss, Dai Li, would visit him there sometime after he got settled during the next few days. After they left him, Wang made his way to Nanjing on a boat up the Yangtse River, thrilled to be back in China and proud that he had already found gainful employment.

Just as the recruiters had told him, Dai Li came to his apartment three days later, taking Wang by surprise by mysteriously entering through the back door shortly after sunset.

"Wang Dacheng, I'm your new boss. I'll be observing you carefully over the next several months to make sure that you are cut out for the work we are going to ask you to do. If I've any doubts, we'll let you know, and you'll be expected to vacate the apartment immediately, leave the keys on the kitchen table, and forget you ever met me or the other two gentlemen. If you meet our expectations, however, and we accept you into our organization, you can be assured that we'll always have your back."

They spoke together for half an hour, as Dai Li laid out a few general guidelines and a training schedule for the next few months, possibly years. Dai Li told him that he, Wang, had been identified by Chiang and Mayling as one of the most linguistically talented agents, so that he would be expected to learn English over the next five years. They would provide him with several good

English teachers once he was accepted into the organization.

Wang swore his allegiance to Dai Li, Chiang Kaishek, and to the KMT party. He promised his new boss that he would never disclose his occupation or his activities to anyone, including closest family members. Wang considered his mother in Beijing and his sister in Shanghai and figured he would have no problem withholding information from both: The less they knew about what he did the safer they would remain. He was not thinking about marriage at the time, so it did not occur to him how hard it would be to keep such a secret from his spouse.

Dai Li was a coarse and largely uneducated man, so Wang played down his own education. In order not to threaten Dai Li, Wang emphasized, instead, his skillset—facility with the German language—which he knew was of great value at that time to the KMT. He would not be showy about his talents, even though he prided himself in his ability to learn new things fast. Wang was especially excited about the opportunity to study English with good teachers in Nanjing. After they covered the basics about the job, Dai Li looked intensely into Wang's eyes, as if to solidify all that they had just discussed. Then, he took out a document and an ink blot.

"Make sure you agree with this and once you agree, you and I will both put down our thumbprints."

The document contained just two lines:

Wang Dacheng agrees to be employed as a secret agent for the KMT, one of the highest and most important positions in the land. His immediate boss is Dai Li, but he will be forever loyal to Chiang Kaishek and to the Republic of China.

Once Wang put his thumbprint on the document, Dai Li did the same. Then, Dai Li took the piece of paper over to the sink where he set it on fire. As soon as the document had vanished, he abruptly turned around and walked toward the back door. Just before exiting the apartment, he turned around and said a final word to Wang:

"One last thing: If you are accepted into the organization, you must be aware that the only way to leave the life of a spy who reports to me is in a coffin."

With that, Dai Li, slid out the back door as unobtrusively as he had entered. Wang's adrenalin was surging, his heart pounding. He took note of Dai Li's parting words and considered them from time to time over the years; but at that moment he embraced the challenges and excitement of his new job. Wang wanted, most importantly, to be accepted by Dai Li and his group.

Wang especially liked his cover: It was a job for which he felt suited and would have aspired to at a different time. He discussed it, even embellishing on the phony job description with everyone, including his family members. In fact, Wang often went to the publishing house in Nanjing and checked in with the owners and all the employees, even helping occasionally when the publisher had a thorny question about translation. The boss at the press must have been visited by Dai Li and been in on the secret because he played along with Wang beautifully every time.

Several months later, an intelligence officer relayed the message to Wang that he had been fully accepted into the organization.

"Boss asked me to give you his congratulations and his welcome."

Wang took the opportunity to travel to visit his mother, and he went specifically to see his sister in Shanghai at least once a year thereafter, to stay for several weeks. He had no problem keeping quiet from them about his real job and his activities with the SSD. As far as his mother and his sister were concerned, he was utilizing his education and his German language skills. Despite her earlier protests about him leaving his law program, his mother was happy to have him back home in China. The only thing she complained about was that he was not yet married.

"Will you let me find a wife for you? That seems to be the only thing keeping you from being happy. I've a friend who has a beautiful, talented daughter your own age who is ready to get married."

"Ma, I think you're right and, in a few years, I'll take your advice seriously about getting married. However, I'll find a wife on my own; I don't need you to assist me."

During the first five years of his new career, Wang was focused, living and working in Nanjing during the glory years of the Republic of China— by day acting the part of a bilingual reporter, and by night or by special assignment carrying out projects aimed mostly at thwarting the Communists. When he spoke about his mission to other agents within the SSD, he would always reiterate his vow that he was assisting his boss, Dai Li, and Commandant Chiang to unite the country behind one KMT flag.

In 1937, after Chiang returned from Xian and agreed to lead a United Front, the SSD was shuttered because of its focus on gathering intelligence against domestic adversaries: Communists and Militarists. However, Dai Li rebranded a new spy organization named Military Statistic Bureau (MSB) with the charge of collecting intelligence for the purpose of resisting the Japanese aggression. Wang and most others working for the intelligence agency were seamlessly rehired into this newly conceived intelligence agency.

Dai Li had proved himself loyal to Chiang ever since he attended the Whampoa Military Institute in

1925. Three years after that, Dai Li proved himself a spymaster during the Northern Expedition in 1928, when he ferreted out information that might assist the KMT in its efforts to rally Militarists around a single KMT flag. Chiang noted that Dai Li was not only intensely loyal but also ruthless, able to carry out high level assassinations.

Chiang's trust for Dai Li increased in 1936 when Dai Li accompanied Mayling to Xian after Chiang was kidnapped by Zhang Xueliang and another renegade general. Contrite for having failed to prevent Chiang's abduction in the first place, Dai Li went down on his knees, apologized in front of everyone present, and took responsibility for the calamitous event. Thereafter, Dai Li was the only person Chiang ever allowed in the same room with him bearing a gun. In return, spymaster Dai Li remained loyal to Chiang until he, Dai Li, died in a plane crash in 1946.

About the same time that Wang began working

for the SSD in 1932, Lei Jun was moving into the dormitory room at Nanjing's Opera House with her new friend Su Ming. As the two teenage girls lay in their bunks at night, they often imagined what kind of men they might end up with and what kind of life they might have in the future.

"Su Ming, you know I hope to marry a quiet, intelligent man, who respects me to do my own business and trusts me to raise kids and run the household."

"Lei Jun, I hope you get the man and life you seek, but it is not easy to trust what people say to you. Sometimes they themselves don't even know what they'll become. For me, I want certainty. I need to know that the man I get involved with is entirely honest with me from the beginning. I do not have higher hopes than that."

By age 29, in 1937, Wang had decided to get married and to start a family, despite his commitment to Dai Li and to the KMT. Moreover, he was certain he could handle both his job and a family. When he was told that he no longer would be working for the SSD, but rather the MSB, Wang took the opportunity presented by the organizational change to challenge the unspoken rule that spies should not get married. Wang would become a successful husband and father in the same way he had accomplished most other endeavors in life. Supporting his decision, his mother in Beijing had been urging him to have a family.

When Wang Dacheng met Mr. Zou at several KMT conferences, Mr. Zou did not know Wang was an intelligence agent, but he knew the government was relying on him for matters regarding his knowledge of German. During one of such meetings, Wang mentioned to Zou his desire to find the right woman to marry, and Zou immediately invited Wang to visit his house in Hankou, where he promised to introduce him to a beautiful young woman named Lei Jun.

"This young woman is talented, good looking, highly intelligent and, like you, eager to get married and raise a family."

Zou had assessed the two young people correctly, and they fell for each other almost immediately. Once Wang had proposed to Lei Jun, and the two had agreed to have a quiet ceremony on Mr. Zou's compound, Dai Li made a point of returning to Wang's flat several days before the wedding. As he had when Wang was first recruited, Dai Li entered uninvited through the back door just after sunset and sat himself down at Wang's kitchen table. Wang was surprised that his boss knew about his marriage plans, for he had been keeping the wedding as quiet as possible. Dai Li did not forbid him from getting married; rather he stressed to his young and stellar recruit the sanctity of spy work.

"You know, agent Wang, I too love women.

And…women can be of enormous help to us when we need information. But, even with a wife whom you love and trust, an agent needs to keep everything secret."

"I understand and can assure you that I'll keep my oath to you, to the Generalissimo and to the Republic of China. This won't be a problem for me."

With that odd exchange about women and marriage, Dai Li slipped out the back of Wang's apartment. As Wang's duties increased, and as he was compelled to travel and to stay away from home for longer periods of time, he told Lei Jun and others that he had taken a new position as a traveling journalist for the same Nanjing publisher. In reality, he was now responsible for covering the eastern seaboard, on the frontlines of the war against Japan.

After the United States and Britain joined China in the war in 1942, Wang began spending weeks at a time far inland in Chongqing, at Dai Li's headquarters known as Happy Valley, where the KMT and US naval intelligence officers integrated their skillsets and techniques for counteracting Japanese aggression. Wang's new work arrangement forced him to split his time between basic spy work and high-level analysis, which he presented to KMT and American policy makers. As a result of his dual responsibilities, Wang suddenly became far more anxious than he had been during his first six years serving under Dai Li. Still, he never discussed with Lei Jun where he was going and what he was doing.

During most of the war, Wang was required to relocate his station every month or two between three important former KMT strongholds: the outskirts of Nanjing, Hankou; and the French Quarter in Shanghai. In order to accommodate his need to work in these three different cities, Wang directed Lei Jun to move between one of three flats, depending on his project and depending on the danger level in various areas at the time. He directed her to move between cities by first dressing up as a fruit seller, but he never disclosed to her why her disguise was of national importance.

On one occasion, during the summer of 1938, Wang directed Lei Jun to relocate to their flat in the French Quarter in Shanghai several months before the fall of Hankou. Months later, she realized that had it not been for his directive, she would have been killed during the Japanese attack on that city. In other words, Lei Jun figured out that her husband had important information about the war—that he certainly knew more than she did about the bigger picture of events.

As the lights in Nanjing city flickered off at the end of the glorious decade, Lei Jun's married life with Wang was starting anew with some hope and enthusiasm: It was certainly exciting for a few years. However, from the start of their union, that hope continuously dimmed by the realities of the war, the demands being placed on Wang at work, and the debilitating silence between them in their married life. Lei Jun trudged through the next decade of her life—between the ages of 20 and 30—trying to be a resilient and supportive wife. Were it not for her love of mahjong, which forced her to focus on something other than her marriage, and which provided her friends and conversation in all four locations they called home during that decade, she may not have remained sane during those turbulent years at war.

Love During Wartime

Lei Jun's departure from Nanjing in November 1936 corresponded roughly with the tragic ending of the city's glamorous decade of growth and prosperity. So it is, that personal drama sometimes echoes political theater on a larger scale. While Lei Jun was living in Hankou with her best friend Su Ming, eager to find a suitable mate, the KMT's future direction was also suspended in limbo. Echoes continued. The terms of the United Front between the Nationalists and the Communists were accepted by both sides about the same time that Lei Jun and Wang Dacheng were married in Hankou. The United Front, as well as Lei Jun's marriage, remained mostly intact until the end of the Second World War in 1945. Both alliances began in earnest, with great promise, and both ended with grave disappointment.

The world events that occurred during this timeline—1937 to 1946—eclipsed everything in their wake. Yet, amidst the tumult, there existed a love story between Lei Jun and Wang Dacheng resulting in the creation of two children who each went on to have extraordinary lives. Their union might have worked well in a different age and time; in the end, their marriage never really had a chance to flourish.

Lei Jun was tall, beautiful, intelligent, witty, and hardworking; most of all, she was ready to be married to a good man and to build a family. Wang Dacheng was also slightly out of step with the times. He was idealistic, erudite, well-traveled, handsome, and sincere. He had dreams of becoming a famous lawyer or judge who would spend his career helping build the integrity of China's judiciary in a post-dynastic world. During his first year of law school in Berlin, Wang yearned to find a wife one day who was independent minded and who would love and support him in his ambition; when he first met Lei Jun in Hankou at the house of Mr. Zou five years later, he was sure that he had met that woman whom he had always dreamed of.

There were two problems preventing the couple from cultivating a strong marriage from the beginning and then from maintaining happiness thereafter. The first, of course, was the war and the external chaos that defined their nearly ten years together. The second problem was the profession that Wang became dedicated to immediately after he returned to China from Germany in 1932. Unknown to Lei Jun until well into their marriage, Wang had taken an oath five years before meeting and marrying her, that he would never disclose his profession to anyone.

Shortly after Chiang, who now representing the United Front that encompassed his KMT troops as well as Mao's Communist fighters, declared war on Japan in July 1937, the Imperial Japanese forces began an onslaught of magnificent proportions. The first battle against the China's United Front was in Beijing near the Japanese stronghold in Manchuria, or Manchukuo as they had renamed it. After taking Beijing and then Tianjin in the north without much struggle, Japanese troops moved to Shanghai, at the mouth of the Yangtse River. The Japanese military was determined to attack until the Chinese surrendered. Unlike in Beijing and Tianjin where the United Front failed to put up much of a fight, Chiang prepared his best forces for battle in Shanghai.

The battle of Shanghai, which took place between August and November 1937, was the largest and bloodiest standoff between the Chinese and Japanese throughout the war, and ultimately resulted in Chinese defeat. While numbers of dead were high for both sides, it was particularly devastating for Chiang and the KMT because they lost 60 percent of their elite forces—men who had been training for several years with the help of German military advisors. Once it was clear that the KMT had lost Shanghai, Chiang ordered the remainder of his troops to retreat. The Japanese infantry, drunk with success, began making their way up the Yangtse River toward the capital city of Nanjing, raping and pillaging along the way.

During the battle of Shanghai, the new bride Lei Jun was spending her time in Hankou organizing neighbors to play mahjong while her husband remained away from the house. Wang, she much later figured out, was gathering intelligence about the intentions of the Japanese as they planned their next assault. He knew sooner than most that Japanese military would continue their attack along the Yangtze to bring China to its knees. Hankou, at that point, was a relatively safe place and remained so until the last months of 1938. During much of that time Lei Jun continued to visit Su Ming and the friends she had made in Mr. Zou's house.

In her own small flat, Lei Jun had set up a small card table in the living room. Once she settled on three partners who shared her own attitude and ability to the game, she closed the front door and calmed her spirit by concentrating on moving her tiles and perhaps making a little pocket money. When Wang did return home during this period, Lei Jun sincerely wondered what he had been doing; he was obviously shaken.

"Where have you been, Dear? Are you alright? Tell me what is bothering you."

"I am fine, I have been working hard on writing an article in German about the War in Shanghai. I witnessed many atrocities. The waters of the Huangpu River are running red with blood from our people...but I really cannot say more about it than that."

While Lei Jun was living in Hankou, starting in December 1937, her city of Nanjing was flattened, first by some 500 bombs dropped by the Japanese air force in preparation for an assault by land. The bombs destroyed much of the infrastructure that had been built up during the prior decade—power plants, water works, radio stations and hospitals--yet it was a two-week assault by troops on the ground in which the Japanese displayed a cruelty that violates all sense of humanity. The capital city of Nanjing had become a jewel of the Republic of China, transformed from a sleepy town before 1926 into a bustling international city by the early to mid-1930s.

Chiang had moved most of his troops out of the city before the assault by land, and so innocent and unarmed civilians were left to confront the crazed Japanese soldiers. The soldiers for a six-week period abandoned all constraints, killing hundreds of thousands of local people in the most horrific ways imaginable. Nanjing's glorious decade ended with grisly finality in January 1938, at the conclusion of so-called Nanjing Massacre.

Lei Jun and her family members had all miraculously exited Nanjing before the Japanese onslaught: Lei Jun herself to Hankou; her eldest brother had moved to Chongqing; her sister joined her husband's family in Guangzhou; her younger two brothers, Huifeng and Chaofeng, were studying in boarding schools outside the city; and her mother and father were staying with her mom's relatives in Yangzhou. By December 7, Chiang and Mayling, too, had left Nanjing by flying west to Lushan. As soon as Chiang heard word about the impending infantry attack on Nanjing, he had given orders to relocate the entire KMT government to Hankou, leaving the general population mostly without defenders.

Soon after the violence had mostly abated in Nanjing, at the end of February 1938, Lei Jun made her way to Yangzhou to see her mother, to make sure she was all right. Once she and her mom reunited, Lei Jun was assured that her siblings were alive and well.

"Your older brother left with most of the money we had after selling our house. Huifeng is in Nanchang by now, working as a full mechanic for the air force. Chaofeng is ok, I know, because I heard from a friend who lived down the street that his principal had moved the entire school away from Nanjing before the Japanese troops arrived. Your older sister is in Guangzhou and doing well. How are you, dear? Everybody wants to know."

"I am fine, Mom, but I'm a bit lonely because Dacheng is gone most days of each week. I can't complain, though, because I've made friends in Hankou. I'm getting by, as well."

Following the massacre in Nanjing, the Japanese continued their move up the Yangtze River with the aim of attacking the temporary headquarters of the KMT in Hankou and the surrounding city of Wuhan, Lei Jun's new home. For ten months Hankou had been spared conflict, but in October of 1938 the Japanese Imperial army defeated the United Forces in the Battle of Wuhan, repeating the pattern of destruction begun in Shanghai, moving troops further and further upstream along the Yangtze River.

Once again, Wang had known of the Japanese plans before others and so had directed Lei Jun to resettle weeks prior to the attack on Wuhan. Chiang had begun moving KMT governmental personnel and apparatus to Chongqing once he knew that the attack on Wuhan was imminent. The journey to Chongqing, nearly 1000 kilometers further northwest on the Yangtze River, was a harrowing one, but eventually provided natural protection from the surrounding mountains. For this reason, it remained the headquarters of Chiang's Republic of China government for the remainder of the war.

The Japanese military maintained its goal of forcing Chiang to surrender, despite Chongqing's natural shelters from the caves embedded in the steep canyons. The Japanese continued their relentless attack on the ROC government by utilizing a superior air force. Between 1939 and 1943 Chongqing became the most heavily bombed city in history, suffering over 250 raids, and resulting in the death of tens of thousands of civilians.

While Lei Jun and Wang spent much of the next seven war years in Chongqing, they also traveled frequently to three other cities: Shanghai, Nanjing and Hankou, cities that were now occupied by the Japanese. In Shanghai, they maintained a small flat in the French Quarter, a protected area of the city that remained semi-autonomous from Japanese control until the summer of 1943.

When Wang decided, for whatever reason, that he and Lei Jun needed to move their location, he would send her a secret message via some person whom she had never met. After sundown on any given night, after receiving a cryptic message from her husband, Lei Jun would then dress up as a fruit seller as per her husband's instructions and travel to the specific flat designated in the directive. Sometimes Wang would be waiting for her and other times he would meet up with her several days later.

For the first three or four years, this bizarre life was tolerable for Lei Jun, even exciting. If her husband continued to give her enough money to travel in the safest and most expedient fashion possible, she took on this new life with a sense of adventure. She never knew why she was being asked to move or why she had to travel in a disguise; yet in the midst of the war, everyone around her was simply trying to survive. Lei Jun instinctively determined during those years that she need not know too much about what she was being asked to do.

More than her own safety, Lei Jun became increasingly nervous observing Wang's anxiety about things unknown.

"Why are you so nervous, Dear? What is bothering you?"

"I'm not nervous about anything. It is just a day like any other day. Please don't keep asking me such questions."

To ward off anxiety about Wang's long absences and his continuous silence about his affairs, Lei Jun focused on cultivating and refining her mahjong skills with companions in whatever city she happened to be living. Lei Jun's passion for mahjong grew, as if to shield her from the unpleasantries all around—the death and destruction outside, as well as the excruciating silence she endured. She cherished her sessions at the mahjong table. While she was playing with friends, nothing could disturb her. Moreover, she had trained her partners in each of her four neighborhoods—Chongqing, Hankou, Nanjing and Shanghai--not to ask too many questions about where she had been or why she had been gone for so long.

Lei Jun devised a creative way to handle the danger all around her: the random bombs, gratuitous killing, general harassment. She treated the world around her as if it were a mahjong table; She moved this way or that unemotionally, as if she were moving tiles during a game with cool calculation. In this way she mitigated the fear she felt for herself, as well as being scared that Wang would not return. Once she sat down at the mahjong table, Lei Jun no longer worried. Instead, she was temporarily in control of her space, and nothing could encroach on her sense of empowerment and well-being as she moved the tiles and teased the other three players.

When Lei Jun and Wang secured their flat in the outskirts of Japanese occupied Nanjing in the summer of 1938, much of the city had been destroyed by heavy bombing, including Lei Jun's family home and convenience store. Most of the population, those who still lived inside the city walls, seemed to stumble around listlessly and impoverished, their eyes somewhere else, as if they had died and ended up in hell. The landmarks around Nanjing that had once guided all their lives and given them collective meaning had mostly been demolished. Every person in Nanjing had experienced tragedy—family members killed in horrific ways, homes and businesses obliterated. At the mahjong table, Lei Jun always preferred to divert attention away from sorrows and heartbreak and to direct people instead to mahjong. Lei Jun discovered that mahjong provided her partners enough joy to persevere through another day.

"Your turn, Mr. Xie. Concentrate on your next move; only after you play your move, do I want to hear about your dear wife."

Lei Jun's living quarters in Shanghai were the most cosmopolitan of the four small homes she inhabited during those years. When living in this Shanghai flat, Lei Jun interacted with people from all over the world. Wang and Lei Jun were able to remain in the same flat, undetected, until late 1943, shortly after Bizha was born. When in their French Quarter flat, Lei Jun often played with a group of well-established KMT women, some of whom were wives of officials, some of whom were high-class mistresses, and some might even have been spies. She was often uncertain who they were. Lei Jun was always the youngest, so she chose to stay silent and to focus on the game. The Shanghai ladies were the best players with whom she had ever played, and just sitting at the table with them gave her a rush of adrenaline. She tried hard to not make any mistake, lest she be wiped out.

As Lei Jun used mahjong to numb her fears, Wang became increasingly annoyed with her passion for the game. He would often find the house empty, when he returned after a difficult mission of some kind, hot, tired, and hungry. Lei Jun would be playing mahjong in a neighbor's living room. Sometimes when he returned, she would be hosting a game in their living room. In either case, Wang was dissatisfied. Even though Lei Jun would invariably stop or call off the game and then diligently attend to Wang's needs, she refused to apologize or to substantively give up her mahjong habits. She had determined early on in their marriage that mahjong was literally saving her life by keeping her occupied and distracted from her worries.

"If you tell me when you will return, then I

will be ready for you. But I never have any idea whether it will be six hours or six days. I figure it's better to keep myself occupied so I don't go crazy worrying about you. Surely you understand that don't you?"

"I understand, but it seems that you love mahjong more than you love me or our marriage. What's going to happen when we have kids? Lei Jun, I must move constantly, and some of the time you must move as well. It is for the success of my job that I need you to do as I say, and it will also be for our safety. "

Lei Jun slowly came to know that she was playing a part in a greater drama of some kind. However, as the years went by, she remained never quite sure about the reasons behind any given move, and she grew scared and resentful. By the time she became pregnant with Bizha in 1942, her good attitude had vanished; it was unacceptable, she thought, that Wang was not able to spend more days supporting her, and especially that he was not there to welcome their daughter into the world. When she was six months pregnant with Bizha, she refused for the first time to respond to his directive to suddenly leave Shanghai and relocate to Chongqing. She decided that it was just too long a distance and too difficult a journey to travel alone while pregnant.

Wang first urged Lei Jun to stay with his sister, who lived on the outskirts of Shanghai; however, after seeing the flat, Lei Jun felt there was not enough room in the house. She would have to share a tiny room with two of Wang's nieces, getting no space of her own. Wang then tried to move his pregnant wife to his mother's house in Beijing. This idea also failed to calm Lei Jun's nerves; the north was cold, and she was concerned that her southern dialect was not taken seriously. In the end, Lei Jun determined that she was better off on her own in Shanghai, negotiating with people whom she had befriended since getting married. Her mahjong women friends in Shanghai, it turned out, were everything she could have hoped for: experienced; caring; protective and motherly.

One time, a month or so after giving birth to her daughter Bizha in April of 1943, Wang came back to their flat with the man he introduced as his boss. Dai Li said little but was personable and looked intensely at Lei Jun and at baby Bizha.

"Lei Jun, my name is Dai Li. I told your husband that I wanted to meet you and to see your baby girl."

Lei Jun had heard Dai Li's name many times while sitting at the mahjong table. Even uttering his name evoked fear. He was simultaneously highly revered within the KMT sphere of political influence as a patriotic spymaster. The gossip was that he was not afraid to stand up to anyone and all knew that he was Chiang Kaishek's most trusted bodyguard. It was also rumored that he loved women and, strangely, had soft, manicured hands.

"I am honored to meet you, sir."

"Ma'am, you must move away from Shanghai soon, the French Quarter will no longer be a safe place to be."

As quickly as Dai Li had appeared, he was gone. Lei Jun was shaking, for she now understood everything: Her husband was a spy and had been a spy ever since they were married. Now she knew why he had to travel all the time and why they had to keep on the move. Suddenly she understood why he was unable to talk about anything that he did. She was satisfied and relieved in a way, but also suddenly very worried. Over the next few days, as she processed the information, she felt increasingly misled.

"You should be in Chongqing by now. Why didn't you do as I told you?"

"I have a baby girl to take care of, and I need to be in one place as much as possible. Dacheng,

I am not sure I want to live this life anymore, now that I know what you do. I am tired of always being scared."

That exchange took place in early April 1943. Despite her early defiance to her husband's directive, Dai Li's words convinced Lei Jun that she should heed the order to leave Shanghai. The small family left for Chongqing that night, first Wang and then Lei Jun the fruit seller and her infant baby girl several hours later. By June, just as Dai Li had warned, the Japanese had taken full control of the area once known as Shanghai's French Quarter.

Two weeks after they departed from Shanghai, Lei Jun and baby Bizha made it miraculously to their small flat in Chongqing. Wang had been able to maneuver somehow as a single male and get to Chongqing several days earlier. Upon seeing his wife, dressed as a fruit seller, and his crying newborn, Wang was relieved beyond imagination. They celebrated that night in silence, with a big meal cooked for them by a neighbor. They had no idea how long this nightmare, both on a national level and in their household, would continue. Both had lost any sense of distance between the two worlds: Tumult and calamity visited the collective and the individual without distinction.

In the quiet of the night, when even the bombs and gunshots quieted for a few hours, Lei Jun returned to her conviction that she had been deceived for too long and that she therefore must seek an end to her marriage. She had now been deceived a third time by a man she loved and trusted; this was one time too many. However, the war was in full swing and survival for herself and her baby were, of course, the most pressing concerns each day. Lei Jun and Wang remained married for another four years, but it was increasingly clear, as it was at the national level to those trying to hold together the United Front, that the bond between partners would not hold them together forever.

After the Japanese surrendered in August of 1945, it was not long before the tenuous strands of trust holding together the KMT and the Communists in a United Front fell away and morphed into outright civil war. Similarly, and about the same time, marriage between Lei Jun and Wang Dacheng fell away as well. The people in Chiang's KMT sphere of influence wandered through the next several months not sure whether to be joyful that the War of Resistance was over, or fearful that a new and equally terrifying conflict with the Communists was afoot. Meanwhile, Lei Jun's small family of three set out from one abode to another, far away. Lei Jun was pregnant again and wanted to give birth in Shanghai, soliciting the same friends who helped her when Bizha was born. This time, she did not even expect or hope that Wang would be by her side at the time of delivery.

Walk to the Mahjong Game: Taipei

On this day in early December, at around 10:30 a.m., the temperature is unusually warm. As she always does, rain or shine, Lei Jun puts on a light blue cardigan sweater and pulls out her umbrella from the large vase that holds a half dozen other umbrellas, all lesser quality. Hers is sturdy, with a rubber cap that allows her to lean on it in case she needs it as a cane. Even on a day like this, her umbrella serves as a parasol, keeping the sunlight from directly hitting her face.

Johnny has been ready to depart for several hours, so he swiftly follows behind her grabbing his briefcase and jacket and then locking the door.

"Come on, Johnny, hurry up, I am going to be late."

"I am glad you have your sense of humor back. I was afraid for a while that you would lose yourself in sorrow about Mr. Liu. By the way, how are you going to get back tonight? Should I plan to pick you up?"

"No, I'll get one of my friends to walk me home. Don't worry about me, Johnny."

Johnny and Lei Jun acknowledge the doorman on the way out of their condominium. He is reading the paper, listening to Taiwanese golden oldies, and filling in numbers on a lottery card as a fan rotates above his head, 180 degrees. The mild temperature would suggest that the use of a fan is unnecessary.

Johnny, whose deceased mother grew up in Nantong, located between Shanghai and Nanjing on the Yangtze River, tries to get Lei Jun to reconcile her earlier life with her present existence in Taipei. Much of what he learns by speaking with Lei Jun reminds him that his own mother left the world too early; he now wishes he had had more time to ask her about her childhood.

"Ma, for the last hour or two you have been poring over your artifacts from your earliest days in Nanjing. Don't you find it difficult to understand the world around you here in Taipei?"

Lei Jun looks at Johnny for a second, then, before answering, she looks down, concentrating on the pavement in front of her.

"Listen, the war years were terrible, but I somehow knew it wasn't normal. We were all just looking for ways to survive, waiting for peace again: That's what I remember thinking. You and I are looking at peace all around us. That's all. This is the way the world should be. There is nothing odd about it, nor is it hard to understand. Wartime is what is hard to make sense of."

Johnny and Lei Jun stop at the crosswalk and

wait for the light to turn green. Within seconds they are joined by a throng of others, who all look to be in their early 20s, eager to cross the street. Even Johnny looks old like a dinosaur in this crowd of youth. Lei Jun and her faithful son-in-law maintain their focus on the ground in front of them, and they walk for two more blocks on Zhongxiao East Road before taking a right off the big road onto Lane Number 248 toward her friend's apartment.

Once off the main street, Lei Jun picks up the conversation where they left off.

"Look, Johnny, I'm happy to be able to play mahjong with my friends, the way I used to play with my friends in Chongqing, Hankou, Nanjing and Shanghai. Did I ever tell you how exciting it was to keep moving between various cities during wartime? I was unknowingly living the life of a spy. Of course, I was disappointed and angry once I discovered that my first husband was misleading me for so many years. But I forgive him now. He was afraid he would be killed if he told me anything. How could I stay married to him? Anyway, it was quite exciting to dress up as a fruit seller and travel from place to place. My heart used to pump harder than it does the few times I have gotten four sets of pong in mahjong."

"Watch your step, Ma. I don't want you to get so excited that you stumble...speaking of mahjong, wasn't Soong Mayling opposed to playing mahjong during those days? When you spent time with her, did she ever say anything about mahjong? Did she know that you loved the game?"

"Of course not. We didn't discuss that Johnny. But she had two sides to her, just like most of us do, I guess. She had a public side and a private side. In public, she was against playing mahjong just like she was also against smoking. Who knows what she did in private? I never took her too seriously about such things. Mahjong helped me live my life. Nobody can criticize another human being for finding a way to survive. I know she smoked quite often to calm her nerves, especially during the war. She told people what she thought was best for them and I believe she had a good heart, despite much criticism about her over the years. Anyway, she was good to my husband and to our family."

Johnny is silent as he starts to think about his work at the bank; he barely pays attention to Lei Jun's words. A new management group in his division will assume control today. The bank directors want to implement some new ideas about privatization to their mostly state-run bank. They may want to hear his thoughts about how to inject growth into their stable but anemic revenue stream. Taiwan's economy is stable, but it no longer gives people the thrill that they enjoyed in the 1990s.

This area of Taipei—Dongchu—is already bustling even before noontime. Its popularity has grown steadily over the years since Johnny and his wife bought their apartment 40 years earlier. Back then, their apartment building was on the edge of the city—respectable but still affordable. Now, it is considered fancy, the center of commercial activity. Real estate prices are now out of sight for young families without a lot of money to begin with.

For at least two or three decades, the so-called waisheng people who came from Mainland China in the aftermath of the civil war, people like Lei Jun and Johnny's parents, believed they would be staying in Taiwan temporarily—that they would soon be returning to China. As a result, they did not buy real estate. By the time Chiang died in 1975, and his son Chingguo became president, 30 years of pent-up economic desire from this community in Taiwan—one fourth of the population—resulted in a buying spree of real estate in Taipei City. Taipei was transformed once again as waisheng families collectively realized that they would never return to the birthplace of their parents and grandparents.

Johnny and Lei Jun walk another long block without saying anything to each other. Then Johnny, thinking of his own mother, asks a few more questions that he wishes he could have asked his mother.

"Ma, do you find yourself angry any more...I mean about the Japanese, about the Communists, about the people like my mother who believed that following Wang Jingwei's collaborative government with the Japanese was the best way to save lives?"

"Johnny, I wouldn't be alive if I carried that kind of anger over all these years. Every day I faced small dilemmas: Should I follow my own instinct or follow my husband's directive? Should I leave my kids with my in-laws and exit my own marriage, or should I try to ignore my frustration and fear? You're asking big questions. I could only make the best decision for that moment...The first 40 years were tough, but life worked out for me

 Chapter 10 • Walk to the Mahjong Game: Taipei

finally. All in all, I have had a hard life. I don't wish to spend my last years on earth figuring out who is good and who is bad, who did right and who did wrong...but, it's the little things that still bother me—things done to me by those I cared about the most. I'm still a little upset with my father and that I was tricked by Mr. Liu."

"Yes, Ma, I understand. Sorry for asking you impossible questions to answer."

"Johnny...I am getting excited about my mahjong game. I am feeling I might win today."

"But you still hold anger toward Mr. Liu?"

"Not anger, Johnny. That's too strong. I loved that man once. Anyway, let it go."

Johnny and Lei Jun are still ten minutes away from Mrs. Gu's apartment building. The temperature is perfect, but the sun is starting to feel a little hot. Just as people from a single religious group like to congregate around their place of worship, this area of the city now attracts the best-looking people from Taipei and elsewhere. Young and old gather in these several blocks, especially in the early evening, to be seen by others and to take advantage of sales of brand-name clothing. This is Taipei at its most vibrant and exciting.

In the years after 1949, high quality inexpensive restaurants lined the streets in this neighborhood and especially in the Xinyi area a little distance from Dongchu. There were canteens representing cuisines from all over China, especially the areas where the KMT had been in power: Jiangsu; Shanghai; Sichuan; Jiangxi; Yunnan. Today, those restaurants still exist in the neighborhood, but the successful ones have been passed down to new owners who have adjusted to the changing tastes, localizing their once purely mainland cuisine.

Johnny and Lei Jun are now on the last block of their walk before they reach the apartment where Mrs. Gu and her husband have lived for the past 50 years. Gu Xiaoying has been Lei Jun's best friend for the past decade. She is a 90-year-old lady with a completely full head of white hair, not as tall as Lei Jun. Even at 90, Gu Xiaoying moves with a spring in her step that suggests relative youth.

They reach Mrs. Gu's apartment at 10:50 a.m., with just enough time for Johnny to hail a taxi and get to the bank in time for his 11:00 a.m. meeting.

"You are a good man, Johnny. Perhaps Mr. Liu was a good man too. Thanks for walking me here."

"See you at home, Ma. Hope you win and take us out to eat with your winnings. I want to go to an expensive restaurant this time. You keep promising that, but we never go."

He makes sure Lei Jun is well positioned in front of the elevator, and then turns quickly to return to street. Lei Jun turns her back away from

Johnny, away from the street, and focuses instead on the coming elevator, concentrating on what she will say to her friends when they tease her about being so late.

Disenchantment and Glimmer of Hope

A lack of trust doomed the KMT alliance with the Communists. Much blood and bad-will had been shed between the two groups in the years from 1926 to 1937. Questions arose from the start of their alliance in 1937 about whose soldiers— Chiang's or Mao's—should fight in any given battle; whose were dying in greater numbers on the front lines against the Japanese. As the tortuous years of war went on, the lack of mutual confidence in the other made collaboration increasingly difficult; Chiang and Mao were incapable of trusting each other enough to turn the page and start anew.

The United Front had been literally a shotgun

alliance, brokered after Chiang was kidnapped in Xian in December 1936 and forced at gunpoint to alter his policy. After his abduction, Chiang negotiated the terms of this collaboration with Mao, with both sides of the United Front finally agreeing on one thing: The Japanese posed an existential threat to all of China. So, for a moment in time, their distrust of each other was superseded by a collective desire to save the nation.

Chiang had always referred to Mao and his men as "bandits," and did not believe they could embrace a true alliance. His distrust was validated from the start, as the numbers of soldiers stepping up to face the Japanese always suggested that Chiang's soldiers were taking the bigger sacrifice. Further, Mao continued to refine his propaganda and to recruit peasants from the countryside, even though such recruitment was forbidden according to their agreement.

Mao and the Communist also had reason for

profound distrust of the United Front alliance. Chiang had literally been focused on exterminating Mao and his troops for a decade. That fact made it hard, if not impossible to forgive and forget. By January 1941 Mao's distrust was tragically confirmed when in Anhui Province, Mao's New Fourth Army was surrounded by KMT forces. Seven thousand of 9000 Communist soldiers were killed by massive KMT friendly fire, after which Chiang expressed no regret or condolence. The KMT justification for the slaughter of Communist troops was that Mao's soldiers were insubordinate.

On August 15, 1945, after the United States dropped atomic bombs on Hiroshima and Nagasaki, and after the Soviet Union declared war against Japan, the Japanese Emperor surrendered to the major allies: China, United States, Great Britain, and Soviet Union. It should have been a joyful event for those in China who had fought so valiantly for so long in a war of resistance.

Perhaps, for a short moment, it was joyful for Chiang, Mayling, and a small group of their supporters. Yet, no sooner had victory been declared, than the distant thunder of a new war could be heard.

Whatever relief came briefly to those within the sphere of KMT influence because of the cessation of conflict with Japan was replaced almost immediately by simmering grievances against an old enemy, the Communists. The Nationalists and Communists had spent the last year of the war losing what little trust and love they had between them, even though they ostensibly still represented a United Front. The end of the war became an opportunity for both sides to discard pretense of an alliance and to fully express their respective animosity toward the other.

Simultaneously, in Lei Jun's household, the conclusion of the war should have ushered in a new phase of transparency between husband and wife, perhaps a grand apology and a commitment to start anew as a family, maybe even outside of China. Wang might have argued to his boss that his work was completed, and that he wanted to cultivate a simple life. One would have thought that the work Wang did for the intelligence agency would no longer be needed.

However, Wang did not leave his job. Moreover, his workload seemed to increase, while he became more anxious than he had ever been. In March 1946, he might have had yet another opportunity to exit from his profession after the death of his boss, spymaster Dai Li. Yet, neither the end of hostilities with Japan nor the passing of Dai Li did anything to calm his mind.

"Dacheng, the war is over. Your work should be done. Why are you so nervous now?"

"My boss has died."

"What happened?"

"The reports say that the small plane he was

in went down in bad weather—and we know it has been rainy and overcast—but I keep wondering about all the people who might have wanted him dead."

"I'm sorry to hear that, but that means you're free to leave the agency, doesn't it?"

"It's complicated, and I don't wish for you to get involved. The war may be over superficially, but behind the scenes the stakes have never been higher for our country. Lei Jun, I'm more afraid than I've ever been. Now that he is gone, I have no idea who's my friend. If he were alive, at least I would feel safe—that he would always have my back."

Several weeks after this exchange, when Lei Jun was six months pregnant, she had arranged to play mahjong with some ladies at her friend's flat in Shanghai. Lei Jun had hired a helper to watch over Bizha for a few hours. She returned from a mahjong game, several doors away, and was surprised to find Wang in the house. Bizha had fallen asleep in the same room on a mattress in the corner and Lei Jun turned her attention to her husband. She observed his intense state of agitation. They sat near their bed preparing to sleep for the night.

"I can't take any more anxiety, Dacheng. I have lived in fear most every day and every night ever since the day we were married ten years ago. And the worst of it has been, until Dai Li came to visit us after Bizha was born, I had absolutely no idea what I feared. You refused to tell me anything about where you were going, what you were doing, or when you would come back. If it weren't for mahjong and my friends whom I have had along the way, I'd be crazy by now."

"I'm sorry, dear, but I'm really, really afraid right now."

Lei Jun looked at Wang's face; the color had vanished. She heard keys, which he still held lightly in his left hand, lightly clinging because of his now uncontrollable shake. Lei Jun's eyes followed the direction of his right hand that was resting on the edge of the bed—a straight line from which led her eyes to his pillow. Peeking out from under the lower section of the pillow was the steel tip of a gun. With conviction, Lei Jun abruptly walked to the pillow and turned it over, exposing the revolver.

"You were going to have me sleep with that gun in my bed—with our baby in the same room?"

Wang was silent, his hands still shaking.

"Please take that gun away from here. I can't stand this anymore. There must be a better way to live."

Lei Jun's dilemma now was more complicated and nuanced than it had been with either her father, when she was 15 years old, or Mr. Liu at age 19. These two prior incidents involving men whom she loved but could no longer tolerate, precipitated immediate action. Lei Jun could not pack her suitcase and sneak away the next morning to stay with her best friend, as she had when she was 19 years old in Hankou. Now, Lei Jun had a baby girl to consider. This time, she needed to maneuver carefully. She was not numb or nauseous, as she had felt during her past two disappointments, but she was on heightened alert, needing to act soon.

Over the next six weeks the couple returned several times to the question of Dai Li's death, and the implication it might have on Wang's life. Wang tried to figure out how Dai Li had died.

"I want to know whether or not the plane was sabotaged by the Communists. Or maybe it was the Americans? Perhaps, even by members of the KMT who disliked him...I know he had gotten on the wrong side of the Soong-Kung clan. If my boss had in fact been killed, would those same people be coming after me? That means you and Bizha might be in mortal danger."

Lei Jun chose to act as if he had been talking to her, even though she was not sure that was the case.

"So, you are still frightened, even after the Japanese have surrendered, and even after your boss has been pronounced dead, releasing you from the intelligence agency?"

Wang's hand continued to shake, even harder. Lei Jun had no idea whether he was fabricating conspiracies, or that he failed to share with her vital pieces of information that would justify his new level of concern. She knew that in his present state he was susceptible to conspiratorial thinking. Lei Jun turned to her husband during these days and weeks and tried, as she had on countless times in the past, to calm him down by showing some love.

"Dacheng, perhaps Dai Li was not killed by anybody. It was rainy, windy, and overcast the night his plane went down. Small planes like

that go down in bad weather all the time. And...
perhaps nobody is chasing you. You may, in fact,
be free to walk away from all of this. The war is
over."

Despite her efforts, and her respect for him,
Lei Jun could not revive her feelings or repair her
marriage from that point on. Trust and goodwill
between them had been strained for too long.
Wang understood that Lei Jun was serious about
separation.

"My mom will be able to care for Bizha for a
while. You know, of course, that I've my complaints
about you as well. You play too much mahjong to
be a good mother for our kids. You understand
that I couldn't have been open with you...I just
couldn't be. I intend to go back to Germany
someday, to finish my law degree."

"Well, I am glad you are thinking about
leaving the agency."

"When I first accepted the job, long before

I met you, Dai Li told me I would never be able to leave his organization alive. That didn't bother me until recently. But ever since the Japanese surrendered, I've been resenting his words. Now that he's dead, I am confused. Is someone else in the agency upholding his pledge? ...In any case, I've sent a wire to my mother in Beijing, letting her know that we'll be arriving there as soon as you give birth to our second child and we're able to travel. I told her that you are a good woman, but that we must part. I also sent a note to my agency telling them the same. You and I will have to go together to meet a few people from the KMT when we are in Beijing."

Lei Jun did not argue. She and Wang were in sync; they had struggled silently for so many years that the path forward to separation was an obvious one. As for the custody over the children, Lei Jun agreed that her two kids would be best under the care of her mother-in-law for now. Wang's mother had a house with helpers who could better facilitate their care at this time. Lei Jun planned to visit regularly.

Several months later, in July 1946, Lei Jun gave birth in Shanghai to a good-looking boy they named Tao Lei. As with Bizha, Wang was absent on the day of delivery and for two weeks thereafter. Lei Jun was accompanied during the birth and comforted afterwards by the ladies with whom she had been playing mahjong—a few of whom had returned to the French Quarter after the Japanese surrender. Bizha was old enough to run into and out of the room while Lei Jun was delivering Tao Lei; she knew something important was happening.

When Lei Jun was strong enough to travel from Shanghai to Beijing, the couple proceeded to Wang's mother's house in the countryside, just outside the big city. The next day in Beijing, after handing off the two little ones to Wang's mother, Lei Jun and Wang traveled to the house secretly inhabited by KMT officials. It was an inconspicuous traditional house, with a large courtyard, about three kilometers from the imperial palace.

"Why do we need to meet people from the KMT?"

"They need to make sure that you aren't going to turn against the party after our divorce. You might not be aware of it, but you've imbibed a lot information about our government simply by being married to me."

"I've no problem with the KMT."

"Tell them, not me."

After being led inside to what looked to be a vast basement complex, they were taken through a secret door into a nicely decorated sitting room. Three men and one woman were present who did not introduce themselves. After a long pause, one of the three men spoke.

"Agent Wang informed us that he would like to seek a divorce. This is a sensitive matter to the

KMT because you've been married for so many years and you may be aware of state secrets. Agent Wang has been exemplary throughout his work life under now deceased Dai Li, and our information suggests that you've been a fine wife to him. He informs us that he has never shared anything about what he does each day with you. Is that right?"

"Yes, that is correct."

"The first time you knew that he was an agent for the KMT was when Dai Li came to your house in Shanghai. Is that correct?"

"Yes, that is correct."

"OK, we consider you now divorced. We wish you both the best. No place is safe anymore, so be careful. Agent Wang, you may go but we need to have a few more words with Miss Lei Jun."

That was the last that Lei Jun saw of Wang Dacheng, her first husband and father to Bizha and Tao Lei. After he was escorted out of the house, the group of KMT officials then carried on small talk with Lei Jun, serving her tea and asking her about her family of origin. One of the three men made an impression on her. He was quiet, kind and smiled gently when she looked his way. Lei Jun had just turned 30 years old; this young man looked to be a few years older than she. The oldest man spoke.

"Miss Lei Jun, we wish to know what you think about the KMT."

"I love the KMT. I remember watching the procession of Soong Mayling come to Nanjing when I was eleven years old. I have no complaints about the government, I just don't want to be married to a man who cannot be truthful with me. I am tired of being scared all the time."

"We understand. We, too, are tired; the war has been hard on all of us. Since you mentioned our leaders, Chiang Kaishek and Soong Mayling, we would like to introduce you to young Mr. Ding.

He and his family know the President and Madame Soong well. Perhaps you can get to know each other some time."

The quiet young man who had smiled at her earlier still said nothing to Lei Jun, but he nodded and smiled again sincerely.

Lei Jun was then led out of the house. She had no idea where she was. The gravity of her situation suddenly hit her when she was once again on the street: She was now divorced, and her children were being taken care of by the mother of her ex-husband. She had enough money for the time being, and she had more hidden in her suitcase that was still in Shanghai, but she would have to start spending carefully. Only able to half-cry as she moved her way down the street, Lei Jun had a hard time knowing which way to turn. Sadness, remorse, guilt, and a sense of defeat overwhelmed her. Strangely, however, after an hour of wandering she began to walk with a slight spring in her step as if she had been released—her body instinctively expressing a small amount of hope.

It was the end of July 1946 and for the next three years, Lei Jun visited her kids every other week at Wang's mother's place in Beijing. During the rest of her time, she often went to Shanghai where she was able to stay with Chaofeng. She also visited Huifeng several times in Chongqing, even though it was more dangerous to travel the long distance. Both brothers provided moral support she needed to establish herself as a single woman again and to consider leaving China.

Agent Wang was too damaged by the war and too scared about what might befall him during the aftermath to be concerned with the family he had just lost. Instead, he hastily married for a second time, this time to a younger woman whom he thought would take care of Bizha and Tao Lei. He and his mother were now responsible for his children. After several months, his new wife named Lanfan became pregnant and moved in with his mother in Beijing. As the days went on, it was clear that Lanfan complicated, rather than simplified, Wang's already difficult family situation. Mostly, Lanfan was not happy with the arrangement.

A month before she left China forever, Lei Jun finally met Wang's new wife Lanfan at her ex-mother-in-law's house. It was after this meeting that she relinquished all faint hope for reconciliation.

"Lei Jun, I want to let you know that my son has remarried. I want to introduce you to Lanfan. I am glad that you can visit with each other. She is pregnant and so your children and her child will grow up together."

With the news of Wang's new wife, Lei Jun resolved that she had made the correct decision to seek a divorce, and that she would now have to take any means possible to break with her past and start life anew. As she stood before Wang's new wife, she could not help flash back to her 19-year-old self when she met Mr. Liu's attractive wife for the first time. Like she had done more than a decade earlier in Mr. Liu's vast compound in Hankou, Lei Jun stood stoically in front of Wang's wife, calculating carefully how she might extricate herself from the predicament before her.

On one of her last visits, Lei Jun spent an hour and a half with her children, not knowing how many more times she would see them.

"Mommy, why don't we stay with you and Daddy anymore? Where are you living?"

"Bizha, I miss you too, dear. Life has become uncertain."

"What does that mean?"

"Never mind, Bizha. I need you to take good care of your little brother. And, you will soon have another little brother or sister as well."

The pain of loss and resentment was now eclipsed by the fact that this new young wife might take responsibility for Bizha and Tao Lei along with her own child. Lanfan might be a good and responsible mother in a way that she was no longer allowed to be. As soon as Lei Jun left her ex-mother-in-law's house, she sent a telegram to her brother, Huifeng, in Chongqing, who was working at an air force maintenance facility. He would be able to help her leave the mainland.

Dearest younger brother, you were right. I must leave the mainland. Please make arrangements for me. Lei Jun.

Once Lei Jun had wired her brother in Chongqing and committed to take the flight to Taiwan, she began dreaming that she might run into one of those same four KMT party members who had served to ratify her divorce. She had taken particular interest in their faces at the brief meeting in Beijing—scrutinizing the contours of their foreheads, the thickness of their eyebrows, the size of their ears—in hopes that she might recognize them somewhere. Who knows, she might get a chance to press them about the bigger picture. What had her ex-husband been doing?

Lei Jun wanted somebody to analyze for her what she and Wang had endured as a couple and she yearned to have someone tell her more about her husband's work—what he had accomplished all those years for the sake of the country and for the KMT. She was certain that if she met one of them again, especially the silent one with the gentle smile, that she would boldly engage in such a conversation. This thought was the only sliver of hope that she lived with during those excruciating last days: The government was collapsing all around her, and she was being forced to sever ties with her kids and plan for a future unknown.

Two years after seeing Lei Jun for the last time in the undisclosed KMT hideaway in Beijing, Wang Dacheng was suddenly abducted off the streets in Shanghai by four undistinguishable men.

The friend Wang was walking with was untouched and immediately reported the incident to Wang's mother and to Wang's new wife Lanfan. The incident involving her ex-husband further alienated Lei Jun from her Mother-in-law's household, as it injected into their relations a sense of fear.

Then, slightly less than a year later, in October 1949, as mysteriously as Wang had disappeared, he reappeared again alive. His Communist abductors had been convinced, after 11 months of torture and questioning, that the focus of Wang's intelligence work had been aimed at the Japanese, not at them. He traveled immediately to Beijing to see his newly formed family. Wang showed up at his mother's house in Beijing broken and scared; he announced that the next day he, his pregnant new wife, and the two kids had to leave for Hong Kong. While Wang fled China for Hong Kong with the two kids and his second wife in tow, Lei Jun was already getting settled in Taiwan.

Several weeks prior to Wang's release, Lei Jun had seen her kids for the last time and had taken the long and dangerous journey to Chongqing, where she had boarded a military aircraft arranged by her brother, Huifeng.

Lei Jun received promise of a seat on a military aircraft shortly after sending her telegram. Chaofeng, too, had asked Huifeng to arrange a seat for him as well. Chaofeng was most convinced of all that the Nationalists were entirely on the defensive. During the summer of 1949, when Lei Jun met Chaofeng in Shanghai, they would discuss their anticipated trip to Taiwan.

"We will be joining our KMT brothers and sisters and prepare for the time we can reclaim the mainland. It will be safer for us there; that's all I know, Sis. Don't think too much about it. It is the right thing for both of us to do. I'll arrive there a few weeks before you, so I will prepare a place for you to stay with me."

With hindsight, the demise of the KMT stronghold in China was apparent for all to see long before the end of the war. During the final two years of war with Japan, the Japanese army had made a major assault from north to south in China's hinterland which extended from Beijing southward to Hong Kong and Kunming. This attack, named Ichi-Go, ultimately had no effect on the outcome of the war; however, it further weakened the KMT position in the countryside and allowed Communists to expand their influence and territory while nominally remaining a part of the United Front. Mao Zedong, leader of the Communist Party, successfully projected a message of hope to the beleaguered masses in the rural areas by proposing his policy of land reform: Once victory was achieved, he promised landless and starving peasants that they would be given their own plot in which to grow crops.

The same peasantry, living under Chiang's

leadership in areas governed by the Republic of China, had become exhausted and demoralized. They increasingly viewed the Nationalists generals as cruel, inept, and corrupt. The overall economy in areas of the eastern seaboard where the KMT was in power, was in trouble. Inflation was spiraling daily because of excessive printing of the national currency. Nationalist Minister of Finance, H.H. Kung (Ailing's husband and Mayling's brother-in-law) under Chiang's direction, repaid government debts and bought new military supplies by issuing fresh bills. Some nine trillion yuan were in circulation by late 1946, and two years later, by August 1948, that number had increased to seven hundred trillion.

Several months after the end of World War II, United States President Truman had sent special envoy George Marshall and his wife Katherine to establish themselves in Chongqing with the aim of brokering peace between the Nationalists and the Communists. They inhabited a house next to Chiang and Mayling, while Marshall traveled often to the Communist headquarters in Yan An.

When this famous American general was not conversing with Mao and Communist leaders, he and his wife Katherine ate dinner together nightly with Mayling and Chiang. Mayling delighted them both, as she had countless times over the past two decades when entertaining foreign dignitaries to China. Yet, a new reality had set in for the KMT: Mayling and Chiang were losing their grip on power in China. Thus, these intimate dinners together marked the end of an era for Mayling. Her status that she once held around the world as the "Empress of China" was diminishing by the day. Chiang had been so consumed by warfare that he had no real plan or ability to win the peace and the KMT was rapidly losing favor throughout the countryside.

While Chiang, Mayling, and the KMT should

 Chapter 11 • Disenchantment and Glimmer of Hope

have received more credit than they did for the Allied victory over Japan, they showed little ability or inclination to establish a peaceful aftermath during the next phase, 1945 to 1949. By January 1947, Marshall left China admitting that his attempt to broker peace had ended in failure. The former adulation for the Nationalists from the United States and from other countries around the world quickly turned to ill repute. There was a growing chorus of skeptics—journalists, authors, and politicians—who doubted Chiang's righteous ability to rule China. Mayling's own sense of triumph descended into despair. Curiously, United States and United Kingdom remained nominally supportive of the KMT during the civil war, despite their profound misgivings about Chiang's leadership.

Between 1947 and 1949, the civil war between the Nationalists and the Communists raged. The conflict had begun most fiercely in Manchuria where the withdrawal of Japanese troops created a power vacuum and where they had left a large amount of industrial equipment and weaponry. Under the terms of the Japanese surrender, the Japanese troops were ordered to relinquish all possessions to the KMT and not to the Communists; however, Chiang had few forces in Manchuria, so most of the industrial equipment ended up shipped to the Soviet Union. The weaponry left behind by the Japanese also fell mostly in the hands of the Soviets, who directed it to the Communist rather than to Chiang's army.

In this way, Mao was able to push the Nationalist Army out of Manchuria and Northern China in 1947, setting the stage for his methodical conquest of other parts of China over the next two years. Communist forces grew rapidly during these years for several reasons. KMT conscripts switched allegiances because they were being mistreated, while at the same time millions of landless peasants were taking up arms with the Communists, hopeful, even exuberant, about the possibility of dramatic land reform.

As if to foreshadow the collapse of the Nationalist regime, Mayling had left China in late November 1948 and remained in the United States until 1950, after which Chiang had established his government in Taiwan. Chiang announced his resignation as president of China on January 21, 1949 and Lei Jun's hometown of Nanjing fell to the Communists on April 24 of that same year, marking the collapse of the Republic of China on the mainland. Chongqing fell on November 30, and Mao proclaimed the establishment of the People's Republic of China in Beijing on October 1. Chiang, his government officials, along with approximately two million Nationalist soldiers and civilians, loyal to the KMT, had by then retreated to the island of Taiwan. From the first moment, Chiang maintained that Taiwan was the real China, because, he boasted, the island was being governed by legitimate rulers.

Soong Mayling's departure from China in late November 1948 had signaled the inevitable defeat of the KMT on the Mainland. Mayling lived at her older sister Ailing's residence in New York for nearly two years, despite Chiang's continual urging of her to return and provide support to him and to the country. Not until 1950 did Mayling rejoin her husband—by this time, not in Chongqing or Nanjing, but in Taiwan.

Chapter 11 • Disenchantment and Glimmer of Hope

The Mahjong Table: Taipei

Johnny bids his mother-in-law adieu in front of the elevator that will take her up to Mrs. Gu's fifth floor apartment. Usually, Lei Jun chooses to walk slowly up five flights of stairs. Today, however, she is late, so she waits for the slow, cranky elevator to deliver her in slightly better time to Gu Xiaoying's front door. Lei Jun enters the apartment easily, as the door has been left ajar. She takes off her jacket and puts it on the coat rack, places her umbrella in the cylindrical ceramic container containing other umbrellas next to the door, and finally takes off her shoes, replacing them with indoor slippers that she has left in a special place designated for her on

Mrs. Gu's shoe rack.

Lei Jun and Gu Xiaoying smile broadly at each other and lightly embrace. Over the past ten years Mrs. Gu has become like a sister to Lei Jun, just as Su Ming had filled the role of sister for four years at the opera house. Mrs. Gu, 11 years younger than Lei Jun, was born and raised in Chongqing and at ten years of age watched as her hometown became the seat of Nationalist government. She remembers the frantic way that the KMT government entered the city and seemed to build it up overnight. Mrs. Gu still has nightmares about the Japanese bombing raids that began in February of that year and continued for the next five years. The Japanese air force had persisted with even greater ferocity than what they had unleashed in Beijing, Tianjin, Shanghai, Nanjing and Wuhan.

At age 18, Mrs. Gu married a young man in the KMT air force who took her to Taiwan three years later, in 1949. They lived for the next nearly

60 years together, raising two children, before he passed away ten years ago. After her husband died, Mrs. Gu, at age 80, met a soul mate in Lei Jun. Both ladies share a love for mahjong, good food, and friendship. Each of them has a highly tuned sense of humor and an appreciation for another time and place on the mainland—when the horror of war shaped everyone's reality.

"We've all been waiting for you, Grandma Lei Jun. We were about to come over to your house to make sure you were all right."

"I'm sorry I'm late; I got caught up in my past this morning, looking through my keepsakes and battling with my son-in-law Johnny."

Lei Jun sits down in one of the six comfortable chairs with soft pillows that form a ring around the perimeter of the room. In the center of the room is a card table and a mahjong set. It is their ritual, no matter how late in the day they get started, to sit together and chat for a few minutes before starting a game. The maid brings Lei Jun a cup of tea and Mrs. Gu sits down next to her.

Jing Taitai and Ms. Xie are both considerably younger and are good friends, outside of their games of mahjong. Jing Taitai is only 80 years old and Ms. Xie is 68, a few years older than Lei Jun's youngest daughter Angela. Neither Jing nor Xie seem fazed that Lei Jun is over an hour late; they have plenty to talk about. The two ladies finish up the topic that they have been animatedly discussing, then turn to the two other ladies. In her strong Jiangxi accent, Ms. Xie jumps into the conversation.

"Grandma Lei, what took you so long? We were thinking that you might have forgotten that we were playing today. Also, we were discussing your life a little earlier. You need to tell us again how you met your husband number two, the honorable Mr. Ding."

"Stop teasing me. I didn't forget our game.

I got in an argument with my son-in-law. He still wants to advocate on behalf of Mr. Liu, the man who took me from the opera house to Hankou when I was 19 years old. Johnny doesn't even know Mr. Liu, but the two are similar in many ways. Both are so arrogant."

Jing Taitai knows her friend well and anticipates her bluster.

"Grandma Lei, Johnny is good to you: You know that. I've never seen a son-in-law so attentive and caring. Your daughter married well. Look at you. We all aspire to be like you one day."

"Hm. I guess Johnny is decent, but he certainly knows how to agitate me. I was going through my mementos...Anyway, sorry I am late. Let's play. You all are in trouble today; I feel like I'll win big."

"There Grandma Lei goes, like usual. Almost 103 years old and she still has such passion to win a few hundred kuai off us. Remarkable."

For the last few years Gu Xiaoying has been the primary hostess for their games. When Mrs. Gu's husband died, he left her a sizable amount of money. Her son and daughter live in the same condominium building and remind her that she has plenty of money—that she should be generous with her friends. Her daughter's daughter, 25 years old, already has a two-and-a-half-year-old son, who often makes a presence during the games. He both delights and terrorizes the old ladies when he runs around while they are trying to concentrate.

Mrs. Gu is a wonderful cook whose greatest joy now is planning the menu for their mahjong gatherings. She has taught her helper to produce almost all her favorite dishes. Still, Mrs. Gu oftentimes decides to go around town to specialty restaurants and to pick up this or that dish, depending on her theme of the day. On this morning, she has planned to present her friends with Sichuan food, two of the dishes prepared in her own kitchen under her supervision and two dishes bought outside at her favorite restaurant.

"Sometimes I think that you all let me win because I am so old, and you know how much I like to win."

Jing Taitai quickly responds: "Nonsense, Grandma Lei. If you think that I like to let you win, you don't know me very well. I'd love to win every game, but unfortunately, I can't always make that happen."

Ms. Xie is almost always the one who ends up paying out the most. Next is Mrs. Gu, who clearly plays to entertain and delight her friends with her food. Jing Taitai wins most of the time, and she cares about winning as much as Lei Jun.

The four women get up and move to the mahjong table at the same time, as if inspired all simultaneously by an outside force. Beyond just sharing a sacred time and place, the way soldiers feel when they meet each other after many years, they have studied each other's moves quite well. Each one chooses a seat at the mahjong table, according to their own inclination: "Moving the wind" as they call it. Two more actions, involving both mahjong tiles and the rolling of dice, determine how they should modify their chosen seats. Jing picks one of four tiles that is face down, she then rolls the dice, from that determines which seat she needs to occupy. The other three players subsequently roll the dice, determining where they will sit. In the end, their seat is in part determined by chance, or by forces bigger than themselves. This seat will be theirs for the remainder of their session.

Lei Jun smells the air with deep satisfaction. The pleasant odors from the kitchen are distinctly Sichuan dishes from Xiaoying's native province. Being able to identify the dish, and then to scrutinize the ingredients, is as important to all three ladies at the table as saying, "How do you do?"

"Xiaoying, your sliced fish in hot chili oil smells wonderful. Did you cook those dishes yourself?"

"No, I got Si-Ying to help me. Two of the dishes I bought at my favorite place. You know, I took you there one time. I know the chef."

Lei Jun begins each game with a silent meditation on her past: She thinks first about the back room of the opera house in Nanjing, when she and Su Ming were teenagers charged with filling the teacups of the players. Next, she reflects on when she was in Hankou on Mr. Zou's estate, with Su Ming and Mr. Zou's two distant relatives. Then, Lei Jun focuses on the period just after she was married when she was traveling incessantly between Chongqing, Hankou, Nanjing, and Shanghai. Finally, Lei Jun concentrates on what it was like to play mahjong in Shanghai, in the middle of the French Quarter; the older ladies she had admired greatly and then relied upon when she gave birth, first to Bizha and then to Tao Lei.

Mrs. Xie, a small restaurant owner, is always in a hurry to get the game started, as if she is preparing for hungry customers.

"Come on, I am the youngest here, by a long shot. I think it is only right if I win today. What do you say, Grandma Lei?"

After all her guests are gone each week, Mrs. Gu sits with her helper, and sometimes her daughter as well, and discusses what dishes she will present to them upon their next visit. She is not nearly as keen a player as Grandma Lei or the others, in part, because she is so concerned with her meal preparation and making sure that each of her guests is happy. Jing Taitai is always interested in hearing stories from Lei Jun and Gu Xiaoying.

"Tell us again, Auntie Gu, were you actually born in Chongqing, or did you just end up there for the war years like most everyone else."

"You know that, Xiaomei. I am a native of Chongqing. Most of my family was killed during the bombing raids. I survived with my older brother whom you have met. Oh…you hear me tell you every week."

Ms. Xie is understandably more energetic than the others but still loves playing with the ladies a generation or more older than she. Jing Taitai is an 80-year-old retired schoolteacher, whom everyone refers to as Xiaomei.

Halfway through their all-day session, the mahjong players take a break and move to a long dining table in a different room of the apartment. Ms. Xie, like Jing Taitai, is interested in Lei Jun's marriage, how she managed to be so close to the first lady.

"Tell us again how you met Mr. Ding."

"Well, I was going through a divorce and one of the three men representing the KMT in

Beijing happened to be my future husband. Of course, we didn't know each other at the time; we just smiled at one another and I did not see him again until after I had arrived in Taipei three and a half years later. Once we did meet again, we were instantaneously attracted to one other. It was as if we had both been waiting for that moment."

"Very romantic, Grandma Lei."

Fresh Start

"Hurry up, Miss. Get on the plane. That is a fancy suitcase you have there—like a small chest. Put it over there with the other bags. I'll make sure it gets on the plane in good shape."

Thanks to her brother, Huifeng, Lei Jun was able to board a military plane in Chongqing bound for Taiwan in September 1949, several weeks before Mao Zedong announced in Beijing the founding of the People's Republic of China. The other passengers were young male KMT military personnel who were pleased to be joined by an attractive young woman. In the last days leading up to her flight to Taiwan, Lei Jun was ecstatic to be given another chance in life, somewhere entirely different—a place that might promise relative safety and give her emotional distance from her personal worries.

A little over three years had passed since her formal divorce proceedings in Beijing in front of a tribunal of four KMT officers. Since then, Lei Jun had been restlessly traveling between Beijing, where her two young children remained with Wang's mother, and other cities in KMT friendly areas: Chongqing, Nanjing, Hankou, and Shanghai. In all these places she relied on family members and friends she had made while playing mahjong. Over the eight-year period during the War of Resistance against Japan, Lei Jun had traveled inconspicuously between these war-torn areas; she was as intrepid as any young woman could be.

Lei Jun met Chaofeng in Shanghai several times during that period and she saw Huifeng, who lived and worked at the KMT air force maintenance compound in Chongqing, two times prior to boarding the plane on his compound. She also communicated with Huifeng regularly by telegraph and by letter throughout the period. Both brothers listened to Lei Jun's concerns about leaving for Taiwan without her two kids. Despite her misgivings, they both urged her to accept a seat on a military aircraft flying to Taiwan. Huifeng was especially adamant about leaving the mainland, arguing that the future of her kids in Beijing would be better without her than with her.

"I'm arranging a flight for both you and our brother Chaofeng. He will fly out a few weeks before you. I think that is the safest thing to do. If the Communists were to find out more about Wang's activities—and they will find out!—I am not sure what would happen. Your kids will have a chance in life with Wang's mother and his new wife. From what you told me, Dacheng never disclosed to either of them what the true nature of his work was after he returned from Germany. So, they should be safe from all scrutiny."

Once Huifeng had confirmed a seat, Lei Jun immediately went one last time to see her kids—to be certain that she was making the right choice. If she had doubts, she could have foregone her trip on the day of departure. However, the information Lei Jun acquired during her last visit to Wang's childhood home in Beijing convinced her that she must fly to Taiwan: Wang had a new wife with a child on the way. She had no idea what to expect--nobody did at that time—but it had become clear that she had to leave.

As Lei Jun found her seat on the aircraft she replayed once again her last visit with her kids at the house of her ex-mother-in-law. Wang's new wife had been visibly pregnant and fidgety, and his mother had been nervously pulling at her apron strings. The disheveled condition of the two women who greeted her mitigated Lei Jun's anxiety, even though it would be her last visit. Wang's mother spoke first.

"The children are in the back yard, being watched over by our helper. Up until now we have not said anything to them about their father. Go see them; Bizha is eager to see you."

After a few hours in the garden with Bizha, aged five and three-year-old Tao Lei, Lei Jun considered carefully how she should depart. She generally had complete control of her emotions. Perhaps this was a skill that she developed since age 15 when she began facing her father's addiction, or perhaps it was a style she refined at the mahjong table. In this case, however, Lei Jun collapsed in front of her children. They had no idea what was the matter—that this would be the last time they would see their mom. When Lei Jun got control of her emotions, she moved inside to talk to Lanfan alone for a few minutes. Wang's mother had left the room to attend to something elsewhere.

"You needn't mention to others what I tell you, Lanfan, at least not immediately. I won't be back again. I'm entrusting you to take care of my children as if they are your own. I've no more reason to be at this house, aside from seeing my children. I wish you the best with the birth of your child. Please treat Bizha and Tao Lei well."

Lanfan was aloof and respectful. She had heard what Lei Jun said, however, she was overwhelmed. Nine months earlier her new husband had been abducted and was being held somewhere unknown; perhaps he was dead. Her baby was on the way; now, she had just been entrusted to take care of two children without any real choice in the matter. Lanfan froze, unable to speak, even to ask questions that were obvious and essential about their future. Wang's mother entered the room, just in time to take control of the conversation. Lei Jun gathered herself and decided to continue with her plan.

She departed Beijing and two weeks later, Lei Jun woke up early on the air force base in Chongqing, packed her last remaining items inside her small chest-like suitcase and accompanied Huifeng to the airfield. She was numb, not knowing what to expect in the days and weeks ahead. She had buried all doubts, convinced only that she had to leave the mainland.

Lei Jun observed the faces of the young men she was riding with on the plane, as if her attention to detail was enough to inoculate her from the unknown that lay ahead. In a last moment of panic, just prior to lift off, Lei Jun recalled leaving home at age 15, and then...she remembered the carriage ride from the opera house in Nanjing to Mr. Liu's compound in Hankou...she also pictured Wang Dacheng's shaking hand that led her eyes to a pistol that mostly lay beneath his pillow on their bed.

Her self-musings were interrupted by a soldier sitting across from her, on the opposite side of the cargo plane.

"Hey, Babe, why don't you come over and sit by us."

"Knock it off. Her brother is the mechanic who made sure this plane flies us to safety. Give her a break, would you."

Lei Jun sat motionless for the three-hour flight. However, what began with fright slowly morphed into euphoria. She was leaving behind forever the bundle of fear, anger, shame: Her father comatose on a couch; Wang Dacheng's scolding finger for playing mahjong; a pile of rubble where her home in Nanjing once was.

Huifeng was now a mechanic in the ROC air force. He began as a trainee and then graduated, and for ten years became a full mechanic. After Lei Jun's divorce was formalized in July 1946, she visited him and had remained in close touch ever since. Starting in the summer of 1948, Huifeng began suggesting that Lei Jun fly to Taiwan, where she would be safer.

"What about my kids?"

"According to Dacheng, he divorced you, right? So, you would have to kidnap your own kids if you wanted to bring them to Taiwan with you. That would be exceedingly dangerous and wouldn't be the best thing for the kids."

"But I need to tell you something I learned late in our marriage. Dacheng was a spy; he worked for Dai Li. I know you will treat that information with the utmost care; You, too, work for the KMT military."

"I see. That does add some complexity. Do they know about their father? Does Wang's mother know what he does?

"No, I don't think he told anyone. He would never have told me either except that one day his boss came into our house and introduced himself. Then, I started putting everything together and there was no way that Dacheng could avoid answering my basic questions after that."

"In this case, you must go to Taiwan, and you should leave your children here with Dacheng and their grandmother. They should be safe as long the Communists don't get ahold of you and make you tell them what you know."

By the time Lei Jun boarded the plane, she also informed Huifeng that Dacheng had remarried and that soon after that, that he had been kidnapped on the streets of Shanghai. Huifeng was now more convinced than before that Lei Jun was doing the correct thing to leave for Taiwan as soon as possible.

It was 10:00 a.m., the sky was blue and within an hour after liftoff the army men were collectively painting the picture of what they all might expect on the beautiful island of Formosa.

"I've heard the island we are going to is

paradise."

"I don't know about 'paradise.' I'm sure there'll be problems for us. That's the nature of life, isn't it? Besides, we won't be staying there long. As soon as the Generalissimo has a plan, we will return to reclaim the mainland."

"I've also heard we are going to paradise: Fruit and warm weather; beautiful women. I think I am the luckiest guy in the world, but I had to leave the rest of my family behind."

Lei Jun just listened to the others and did not contribute to the general conversation. She was intensely interested in what they knew about Taiwan and about what they expected once they landed. If all went as planned, she would be greeted by Chaofeng at the military airport in Hsinchu. He had arrived three weeks earlier and promised, before he left Chongqing, to find Lei Jun a safe place to stay, at least for a while, until they both got reestablished.

By the end of the three-hour flight, Lei Jun was calm about her decision. She deboarded along with the plane full of soldiers and walked slowly to the terminal. She felt the warm air, smelled the sweet breeze, and spotted Chaofeng in the corner of the throng of people eager to greet oncoming passengers.

"Sis, sis, over here. You made it. Welcome to Taiwan. I have a small bed for you in the room that I am renting just off the military base. I can't wait to show you around. The place is clean, the food is fresh, the fruit is special. We might want to head to Taipei in a couple of days, once I make sure we have a good place there. We need to retrieve your suitcase."

Two days later, Lei Jun and Chaofeng got a ride into the center of Taipei City, where the Japanese had for 50 years controlled the government. Taiwan was different place than any place Lei Jun had seen on the mainland: the history, the people, the cuisine, the atmosphere. Most of the waisheng people like herself (those coming to Taiwan from Mainland China during those last months of 1949) tended to congregate around the same areas that were protected by military. There were street vendors from different mainland provinces; she heard accents from various places around China all concentrated in this small area. There was a general buzz of excitement. Lei Jun was alive again, as she had been when she was playing on the street of Nanjing at the age of 10.

Two weeks after arriving in Taiwan, and a few days after moving into a new flat in Taipei City, Lei Jun and Chaofeng were invited to a dance by a young soldier whom they had just met. The three set off to a dance hall several blocks from their dormitory. There was magic in the cool Taipei air and she threw caution and modesty to the wind. Lei Jun danced with several young men her own age as well as a few older men. Just before she and Chaofeng left the dance hall, she was approached by a modest man a little older than she. She did not even investigate his face at first, until halfway through the song.

Lei Jun's heart stopped when she recognized the man with whom she was dancing. It was the quiet one who had attended her divorce proceedings, who had smiled at her gently. She would never forget his face. Her original purpose for remembering this man's features was to identify him to ask him about Dacheng; at the time of their separation, she was hungry for insight into her marriage. Three and a half years had blunted the pain that she had once felt. She suddenly saw this man as someone special from her past— a person who might make her whole again. They said nothing to each other and when the music stopped, he turned away from her, embarrassed that she had recognized him so definitively, and that she had such strong feelings associated with her recollection. He was concerned that he might have triggered bad memories. However, after two steps away, he turned back:

"I know where you and your brother are staying. Can I pick you up tomorrow for tea and a walk? How about 3:00 p.m.?"

"Yes, of course, I'll be waiting for you."

Lei Jun said nothing to Chaofeng as they walked back to the dormitory. Her heart was singing, the moon bright, and the stars shone with the promise of a new beginning.

The next day she told Chaofeng about her date with the man at the dance. He smiled, knowing well his older sister's charisma and charm, especially with men. It was Lei Jun's earlier admirer, Mr. Liu, who had saved his life by getting him admitted to a high school outside of Nanjing. And it was Mr. Liu, out of love and affection for Lei Jun, who had helped Huifeng be admitted to the air force maintenance academy.

"Sis. I am glad you had such a good evening last night."

Early Years

Lei Jun and most of the two million mainlanders migrating to Taiwan arrived in 1949 hoping for the best. They fled war on the mainland and anticipated that they were arriving in paradise, but they also believed that it would be only a temporary visit before returning to claim what was justly theirs. To a large extent they were correct about Taiwan; it was an island oasis, separated and mostly protected from all that they had experienced in the mainland. Yet, from the perspective of the islanders who were already on the island— aboriginal peoples, Hakka and so-called Taiwanese—the entry of the waisheng people was, except for a few, disruptive; for some, the mass migration of waisheng to the island was horrifying.

Debate in Taiwan has persisted for more than 70 years about what exactly transpired during those confusing years between 1945 and 1950. The most vociferous disagreements are made during election times every four years and annually on February 28, the day of remembrance of the 228 Incident of 1947.

A year and a half after the Japanese surrendered to the Allies, Chiang's regime was charged with the duty of assuming temporary governance over Taiwan. Chiang appointed General Chen Yi, who originated from Zhejiang Province and married a Japanese wife, thus appearing to be both loyal and sophisticated with matters involving the Japanese. In fact, Chen Yi's appointment in this position was disastrous and resulted in a massacre of upwards of twenty thousand local people that has yet to be forgotten.

The flashpoint of the 228 Incident occurred when a KMT policeman struck a street vendor selling contraband cigarettes who had refused to pay tax. Crowds of locals supported the vendor and the next day General Chen Yi used his police to violently suppress the small protest. He then secretly called Chiang for reinforcements from the mainland. For three weeks, starting on February 28, Chen Yi's police force and Chiang's reinforcements from the mainland killed citizens from all over the island, many of them elites who had been trained under Japanese occupation. With the help of Chiang's National Revolutionary Army, the soldiers continued to brutally suppress the incensed islanders, systematically targeting those whom they claimed were sympathetic with prior Japanese colonialists.

Despite this stain from two years prior, and the simmering conflict that existed as a result,

Lei Jun and other waisheng people saw Taiwan as a relatively peaceful and harmonious place. From the first day she set foot on the island in September 1949, 32-year-old Lei Jun marveled at the beauty and comfort she felt upon arrival. She had witnessed so much violence at the hands of Japanese troops—Nanjing and other cities ripped apart—that it was difficult, at first, to appreciate the odious nature of military rule over locals, which they inevitably linked to Chen Yi's actions two years earlier.

Locals soon were united in their belief that they had enjoyed more respect and freedom at the hands of Japanese colonial rulers, than they were experiencing under KMT rule. Lei Jun and others, over the next decade, believed that they would return to the mainland. They never embraced this notion that, in fact, became reality: The KMT would never attack and reclaim the mainland, and Taiwan would remain their home for the rest of their lives.

When Chiang formally assumed leadership again of the Republic of China in January of 1950, this time in Taiwan, he maintained the status quo of martial law that had been established by his infamous general, Chen Yi. Chiang enforced an iron grip over the island until his death in 1975—a period known as the era of "white terror." For the first decade, the KMT's treatment of locals was heavy-handed, claiming that certain Taiwanese were "Communists" or "Japanese sympathizers." Chiang's son, Chingguo, who served as the head of the secret police until 1965, executed or incarcerated those he deemed treasonous, taking them to prisons on the smaller outer islands. Taiwan citizens today still passionately debate those events of the first decade.

Lei Jun's first three months on Taiwan soil were euphoric. After two weeks in Hualien, she and her brother moved to an insular area in Taipei

City and were thrilled to find others from nearly every province represented. There was poverty and hardship, but also an infectious enthusiasm that poured into the streets of the small waisheng area. The two siblings were able to talk at length again in a safe environment, filling in the pieces of information about their family that one or the other had lost track of over the prior 15 years.

Taiwan quickly became a symbolically exalted place that allowed Lei Jun to heal psychologically and to give her rebirth of a kind. She remained appreciative and hopeful, despite the continual governmental message that the ROC might re-engage in a full-fledged war with the Communists at any time. For the first decade of Lei Jun's life in Taiwan, hostilities with the Communists remained ongoing; Taiwan's air force bombed mainland cities while Mao's forces prepared for an imminent attack and eventual takeover of Taiwan. However, in the quiet of some evenings, and increasingly over time,

Lei Jun maintained distance from what she had witnessed and experienced on the mainland, and in this way was rejuvenated.

For Chiang and the leaders of the KMT who had just established themselves on the island, geopolitical concerns were more important than were relations with local people. Most importantly, a new urgency about North Korea was issued by the United States. In early 1950, Truman had announced that he would not support Chiang's regime in Taiwan because he considered Chiang incompetent and his regime hopelessly corrupt; yet, less than one year later Truman had changed his position entirely. By the second half of 1950 his overriding concern had become the rise of global Communism—a broadly articulated notion that implicated, as adversaries, both the Soviet Union and China. Truman was suddenly reaching out to the KMT for help in stemming what he perceived as new aggression from Mainland China, manifesting itself on the Korean Peninsula.

When Lei Jun first arrived on Taiwan soil, she and others understood that they no longer resided on a vast seemingly endless landmass, but rather on a small island with an entirely different ethos. Slowly over the years she learned about the island culture in the same way that she had learned about secrets on the mainland 15 years earlier, by hearing stories while playing mahjong. Most challenging, waisheng people had to confront the perplexing fact that Taiwanese locals—other Han Chinese—were shunning them. Instead, many locals, were admiring of Japanese culture: food, music, alcohol, language, and aesthetics.

When the North Korean army crossed the 38th parallel in June of 1950, United States military leaders concluded that they needed to take a strong stand in Asia, to stop the tide of Communism and, at the same time, to control Chiang and the KMT from attacking Mainland China. The consensus suddenly became that Chiang was admirable for his longstanding antipathy toward Communism. A new surge of anti-Communism in the United States, as well as the outbreak of war on the Korean Peninsula, changed everything for Chiang—perhaps saving Taiwan from annihilation by the Communists. The United States required an outpost and an ideological haven in Asia and the island of Taiwan was perfect. The timing was good, for the ROC needed outside assistance and foreign aid.

Within a week of settling into her new dormitory in Taipei, Lei Jun had set up periodic mahjong games with others living in the same neighborhood. The casual conversation around the table during that year usually focused on the same theme: Be prepared to return to families and friends left behind in China.

"We shouldn't get too settled here; it could be any day that our soldiers reclaim the mainland."

"You heard the radio address yesterday, didn't you? Our president stated that 'We are a dedicated people and we will be returning to our homes soon.'"

By the end of her second month in Taiwan, Lei Jun had already visited several times with the quiet, unassuming KMT official, Mr. Ding, whom she had first encountered in Beijing and then again, surprisingly, on the dance floor right after arriving in Taipei. While equally attracted to one another, both Lei Jun and Mr. Ding, for different reasons, were cautious about rushing the progress of their romance. Lei Jun wanted to make sure he was exactly who he claimed to be, and Mr. Ding did not want to disclose information too readily about his sensitive job.

It was reassuring to Lei Jun that Ding Yuji knew of her past and that it did not deter him. She did not have to explain to him the pain she intermittently felt for having left her two kids with her former mother-in-law in Beijing. He seemed to understand her anguish and self-doubt. He had already heard about why her previous marriage was intolerable; he seemed to understand her lingering anger and frustration.

Ding Yuji was a quiet, taciturn man who was two years older than she. Often, during midday, he walked with Lei Jun around the campus of National Taiwan University. This was a beautiful pristine campus, which had previously been established in 1928 by the Japanese as Taihoku Imperial University. Lei Jun and Yuji would stroll leisurely around the pond and around the grassy wooded footpaths. She attempted not to discuss her past life, but when she mentioned something related to China, he just listened. She figured that he must have known more about Wang's duties as Dai Li's agent than she did herself. As the days went on, she cared less urgently about what had transpired on the mainland and more about her new life in Taiwan.

Lei Jun was initially more concerned about Ding's silence regarding his own professional life, than she was concerned about his reticence about discussing details about her past. Like Wang Dacheng, Mr. Ding did not want to talk about his job or where he came from, so Lei Jun became suspicious after their third meeting. One day as they walked together on the campus, she finally garnered the courage to take the issue directly.

"You still won't tell me what exactly you do. Are you a spy like Dacheng was? You know that I can't tolerate that level of secrecy."

"No, I can assure you that I am not an intelligence agent. I am just not ready yet to disclose to you what I do. Now...are you hungry? Let's find something to eat."

"Wait, before we get something to eat, can you assure me that you don't have a wife somewhere on the mainland, waiting for you with or without kids?"

Ding Yuji laughed and said nothing for a long time. Then, with firmness he responded.

"No, I can assure you that I've never married. I have a big family and I'm the youngest of six siblings. I've been too busy tending to my older brothers and my sister to have much time to think about myself. Moreover, as you know too well, we've been at war for so long that I never thought it was the right time to start a family. Now, I have a stable job and some flexibility in my schedule, so I'm interested in settling down and raising children. However, I'm concerned that we may all have to return to the mainland at some point soon. Still, I'm getting older, and I can't put off my own desires any longer. We can never exactly predict what the future will bring."

Mr. Ding said more than he liked to say about anything, but he chose a good time to speak. Lei

Jun had listened carefully, and it was just what she needed to hear in order to be put at ease: He was not a spy, he had never been married, and he felt confident about his present job.

"Yes, let's get something to eat!"

While Lei Jun and Mr. Ding continued getting to know each other during the rest of 1950, Soong Mayling was having to adjust to Taiwan as well, and to redefine her new role in the government. Even her marriage to Chiang had evolved into something new since their dramatic departure from the mainland in November 1948. At the time of her departure, Mayling had been exhausted, ill and despondent and she decided to spend most of the next two years in the United States. During the worst year for the KMT, 1949, Mayling had rested in the comfort of her sister's house on the Hudson River, north of New York City.

Mayling was devastated and depressed to see Chinese killing Chinese in one deadly battle after another. Adding to her general anguish about the civil war were new concerns about the fracturing of her own family. She and Chingling had always been on opposite sides of political matters, yet they had been able to remain close with each other for 20 years. The whole family, two sisters and three brothers, had generally stayed mostly cohesive and supportive of each other ever since the death of Sun Yatsen in 1925, despite the schism between the Nationalists and Communists. Now, all that had changed. Her husband and his son, Chingguo, had forbade the Soong-Kung family from entering Taiwan, and Chiang had publicly broken with Chingling.

While Mayling had been absent from the turmoil on the ground in China in 1949, Chiang had begun leaning on his son Chingguo for advice and familial support. Chingguo chose to investigate for corruption Mayling's family members, the so-called Soong-Kung clan represented by Ailing, H.H. Kung, and their son David. Chingguo's reports elevated him while depressing the status of his stepmother, who remained fiercely loyal to her sister's family. Chingguo succeeded in challenging Mayling's previous standing in the ROC government, so that once in Taiwan, Chiang appointed Chingguo the head of the secret police. Mayling, at the same time, had lost much of her authority within the KMT.

By the time Mayling arrived in Taiwan in 1950, she herself had experienced a most dramatic fall in celebrity status. In 1937, she had once been named by Life Magazine "the most powerful woman in the world," and in 1943 she had been invited by Franklin Roosevelt to stay for three weeks in the United States' Presidential White House while she prepared to address both Houses of Congress. Yet only five years after that in 1948, Mayling was being excoriated by many of her previous supporters around the world for upholding a corrupt family and regime. She retreated from her role as Chiang's wartime partner and confidant, choosing isolation. Three times in 1949 Chiang sent Mayling cables urging her to return to China to join him, and all three times she claimed she was still recovering and required more time with the doctors in New York.

Finally, on January 10, 1950, three days after Truman officially announced he had no interest in supporting Chiang's forces in Taiwan, Mayling decided to leave the United States and join her husband once again, this time in Taiwan. Unlike other trips during the prior decade, the United States government made Mayling pay for her own flight to Asia on a commercial airline.

Mayling got her footing in Taiwan by casting herself now as devoted wife to Chiang and matriarch of the newly established ROC in Taiwan. Meanwhile, Lei Jun and Ding Yuji were falling in love. By the end of 1950, they had broken through their period of caution and were increasingly ready to go public with their mutual adoration. One day in November, during lunchtime as they were strolling around the campus of Taiwan National University, Mr. Ding surprised Lei Jun by proposing to her.

"I am a shy and simple man," he said slowly and with great articulation. "Will you marry me? I am so honored to be with such a beautiful and capable woman as you."

Startled and flattered, Lei Jun grabbed Ding and hugged him with terrific vigor. Passers-by took notice, knowing they were witnessing a dramatic moment of some kind.

"Of course, I will marry you; but I still don't know where you work and live."

"Yes, now I can tell you all about it, for you will be joining me there soon. I am Madame Soong Mayling's private secretary and I live nearby her place in Shiling. I spend much of my day at a government office, and then report to her residence late in the afternoon when she begins her office work. Often, she works late into the night."

Lei Jun froze, unable to take in that information. In her mind, she and her sister were still hamming around in front of their convenience store in Nanjing in 1927 trying to mimic Mayling's American accent:

"Please, dear, may I help you...."

"Are you feeling well? Do you still agree to marry me?"

Lei Jun, for the second time in her life, began to sob uncontrollably—this time tears of joy. It was unimaginable—not in her wildest dreams—that one day she would marry a man in Soong Mayling's inner circle. She had admired and looked up to Mayling since she was eleven years old. The sound of firecrackers blasted inside her head. She paused, regained her composure as she always did in moments of tumult.

"Of course," she said quietly.

Lei Jun and Ding Yuji were married in November 1950 in what was essentially a paperwork wedding in the presence of one sibling from each of their families. On Ding's side was his oldest brother, twelve years his senior and the leader of the family for two decades. On Lei Jun's side was Chaofeng, her youngest sibling and close companion for the past year in Taiwan. Lei Jun was dressed in a simple, elegant, white chipao, while Ding wore a perfectly tailored suit that he had had made earlier that week. The couple answered questions in front of a magistrate in Taipei City— a man who had just come from China, also new to the island. The simplicity of the event did not hide the joy that filled the small room.

Lei Jun beamed and breathed deeply in the cool winter air. She stared at her husband and saw a slightly older, experienced man with great integrity and an honest disposition. She remembered the conversation she had had once, long ago, with Su Ming in the dormitory of the Nanjing opera house.

"Su Ming, I will marry a man like my father used to be...one who is steady, reliable, has a good job and wants to build a family. He must understand how much I will add to his life—how special I am."

"Ha, Lei Jun, the romantic! I hope you won't look down on me if I tell you I don't believe in your fairy tales. Life is difficult. Give me a man who is generous and knows how to take care of me. I won't ask for anything more."

Their ceremonial wedding room was a converted old Japanese structure. Lei Jun, Ding and their two respective brothers as witnesses gathered around the podium where the newlyweds signed a parchment in the gathering of five people. Yuji beamed a smile to his older brother and then at his tall, intelligent, kind, beautiful bride. At 35 years of age, he had no unrealistic illusions about women or marriage, having seen his peers in all kinds of relationships and alliances with women. She was trustworthy, independent-minded and seasoned enough to handle any situation the family might encounter.

Soon after the perfunctory ceremony, Mr. Ding's chauffer took the couple to Mayling's residence in Shiling to receive her goodwill and blessing. Mayling expressed her support for the couple and gave special attention to Lei Jun. Mayling was protective of Yuji and reminded them both that there would be almost no one these days more important to her than Yuji. Lei Jun was unfazed. Mayling warmly escorted the newlyweds out from her residence while Lei Jun radiated joy and goodwill, nodding in agreement to everything Mayling said.

When Lei Jun and Ding Yuji were out of earshot of Mayling, nearly having reached their black chauffeured vehicle, Lei Jun spoke.

"Do you think she knows that I love to play mahjong? She won't penalize you if she finds out, will she?"

"I wouldn't worry about it. She has indeed publicly criticized those who play the game. However, she won't say a thing, I'm sure, as long as we don't criticize her for smoking menthol cigarettes."

He smiled and gently put his arm around Lei Jun.

The Walk Back Home: Taipei

"Thank you, Xiaoying, for another wonderful meal."

"You won again, Grandma Lei. How can you keep winning at 103 years of age?"

"I didn't win that much. As usual, Jing Taitai is the biggest winner. At least, I can tell Angela that I didn't lose; but it's hard to claim that I won. Anyway, I've money hidden away to take them all out to dinner this weekend. Xiaoying, are you sure you and your granddaughter don't mind walking me to my brother's house? I can get a taxi if you are busy."

"Nonsense. I need to get outside and walk a little anyway. As you know, I often walk that way with my daughter or granddaughter... Mrs. Xie and Jing Taitai, we'll see you next Monday, right? We have a little break this time before we play again."

"Thank you Xiaoying for the lovely food. See you next Monday."

It is early evening in Taipei. Grandma Lei now uses her umbrella as a walking stick rather than as a parasol. Together with her best friend Gu Xiaoying, and Mrs.Gu's 20-year-old granddaughter, Lei Jun retraces most of their steps back to Angela and Johnny's apartment that she had taken earlier that day. Chaofeng lives two streets away, directly on the same path. Now, at around 6:00 p.m., the neighborhood has a different feel to it. The streets are just as busy—even more so—but there is a feeling of lightness in the crowd, as if the entire area is giving a collective sigh of relief: The day is coming to an end. Friday-night activities suggest the unknown—conviviality, relaxation, possibly romance.

"Grandma Lei, my mom and grandma tell me that you have had the most exciting life of anyone they know. I am interested in things you did and experienced. You must feel a great sense of satisfaction at 103 years of age."

Lei Jun is silent, barely hearing or taking in what her friend's granddaughter is asking her. The sun is setting, the young people are starting to buzz with excitement about the evening. The three companions, two ancient and one young, walk for a full long block before anyone speaks.

"Grandma Lei, where are you taking them to dinner this weekend?"

"Not sure yet, Xiaoying. Angela is just getting back from visiting her kids in Canada, so she may have a strong preference. I'll wait to ask her where she wishes to eat."

"Were you ever in the war, Grandma Lei?"

Lei Jun may not have heard, or she may be choosing not to answer. The three continue to move in silence for another block. They are distracted by a coming siren on the opposite street. Lei Jun walks this block nearly every day, but she never notices that vendor before who is selling roasted chestnuts. She looks closely at his ancient face to try to determine his origins.

"Grandma Lei, what was it like to know the former president and the first lady?"

Lei Jun finally responds to the insistence of her friend's granddaughter.

"I did my best, dear. I did my best. I had a hard life. I hope yours turns out to be easier than mine was."

"Do you have any advice for me?"

"Stay focused on the small things, like mahjong. You can't control all the chaos around you. Even through the most difficult times, you must always find joy in living another day."

Xiaoying slightly squeezes her granddaughter's hand.

It is nearly 6:30 by the time they amble up to the entrance of Chaofeng's apartment building. The doorman, born in Taiwan with parents originally from Henan Province, greets Lei Jun with a big smile.

"You are here to see your brother. I am sure he is upstairs waiting for you."

"Good-bye Grandma Lei. I'll see you on Monday, right?"

"Yes, see you on Monday."

After a short visit, Lei Jun descends the elevator and begins her two block walk alone, towards Johnny's and Angela's apartment. Johnny happens to see Lei Jun as he walks toward her in the opposite direction, carrying a few dishes from a restaurant near his workplace.

"Ma, I hope you won so you can take us all out for dinner like you promised. But just in case, I brought some food home."

"Well, I won, but not as much as I wanted to win. We can eat your food and I'll still take you and Angela out to dinner after she returns tomorrow night."

"I've been thinking about your friend Mr. Liu all day, Ma. I have some more questions about him."

"Forget it for today, Johnny. It upsets me to remember those days. Let it go. I would rather watch a movie tonight."

They go up the elevator together to the tenth floor, where they quietly set the table so they can enjoy their meal together, Johnny and his mother-in-law, who is 103 years old and still plays mahjong nearly every day.

• Epilogue

Epilogue

Chaofeng:

Chaofeng, the youngest of five, lived near Lei Jun and her Taipei family for more than 60 years. He died in 2019 at the age of 98. He was purportedly a wealthy man and remained devoted to his older sister until his last day.

Wang Dacheng:

As mysteriously as Wang disappeared on the streets of Shanghai in 1948, he reappeared again 11 months later, nervous and traumatized but grateful to be alive. He had been interrogated by Communist soldiers who questioned him about the focus of his intelligence activities. Wang must have eventually convinced them that he had been focused entirely on the War of Resistance against Japan—that he never spied against the Communists. Once released from an unknown location in Shanghai, he made his way to his mother's house in Beijing where he announced to his three young children and second wife that they would be leaving immediately for Hong Kong.

He and his family flew to Hong Kong right after he had been released. They found a small flat in the city. Wang soon left the three kids in the care of his second wife, Lanfan. By late 1953 Wang had abandoned the family in Hong Kong and made his way back to Germany where he was able to complete his law school studies, which he had started but not completed over 20 years earlier. His son, Tao Lei, visited him in Germany during the early 1970s and saw his father's law diploma framed and hanging on the wall of his bedroom. Wang Dacheng died in Germany in 1975 at the age of 63.

Lanfan:

Wang Dacheng's second wife, Lanfan, gave birth to a daughter in September 1949. Lanfan was an unhappy and unwilling mother and stepmother. Soon after their arrival in Hong Kong, Wang left her alone with the three children. Lanfan abandoned the kids as well in 1954, leaving Bizha to care for the younger two children, Tao Lei and Lanfan's child Mimi. Bizha was 11 years of age when she assumed responsibility for herself, her brother, and her stepsister. Despite her rough childhood, Lanfan's daughter Mimi, grew up to become a broadcaster on BBC radio.

Yongfeng:

Lei Jun's older brother, the oldest of five,

helped his mother sell the family property early in 1937 and wisely reinvested it in a small theater in Chongqing. He remained in touch with all his family members for the next 16 years. In early 1953 he sent money to Lei Zhao that allowed her, her son, and their parents to surreptitiously travel from Nanjing to Taiwan, through Hong Kong. After he sent money to Lei Zhao he was never heard from again. He most likely lived out his days in Chongqing.

Lei Zhao:

Lei Jun's older sister, child number two, received money in 1953 from her older brother Yongfeng who was living in Chongqing at the time. She left the household of her husband in Guangzhou after he suddenly died. Taking her 18-year-old son, Lei Zhao first traveled northward to Nanjing, reconnecting with her parents who had moved back to their hometown. With the money provided by Yongfeng, the four managed to travel southward and cross the border into Hong Kong. From there, they found passage on a boat to Taiwan. Once in Taipei, they all settled in with Lei Jun and Ding Yuji. Lei Zhao's young adult son chose to live alone. Lei Zhao became an important part of Lei Jun's household for the next 30 years, keeping the house straight and helping raise Lei Jun's three children.

Lei Jun's mother and father:

In summer 1953 Lei Zhao, along with her 18-year-old son, found her mother and father living in Nanjing not far from where the family grew up. Lei Zhao, whose husband had just died, led the four on the treacherous journey, first to Hong Kong, and then to Taiwan. Little is known about how they were able to get over the border between Mainland China and Hong Kong at that time.

Lei Jun's parents arrived in Taipei in

December 1953. Lei Jun's father was no longer addicted to opium, but his body and mental condition showed deterioration from his long-time addiction. He died 18 months later. Six months after him, Lei Jun's mother passed away as well, in late 1955.

Ding Yuji's oldest brother:

He climbed to great heights in his career as a diplomat for the KMT, during which time he served as an ambassador to the Americans right after the war. He was bilingual in Chinese and English, and a highly respected employee inside the KMT. He introduced his brother Yuji and another brother to Chiang Kaishek and Soong Mayling, both of whom found long-term employment with the famous couple. For some unknown reason, he fell out of favor with Chiang and Mayling, lost his position, and spent his last 20 years living in Lei Jun's household—depressed, drinking heavily each night.

He died in the year 2000.

Ding Yuji:

Ding Yuji remained a quiet, hardworking, and devoted husband to Lei Jun. He was adored by his children, wife, and his employer. Ding died at home in Taipei in 1990, at the age of 75.

Mr. Liu:

Mr. Liu and his household moved with the KMT government from Hankou to Chongqing in the last few weeks of May 1938, prior to Wuhan being attacked by the Japanese Imperial Army. He remembered Lei Jun fondly over the years. After migrating to Taiwan in 1949, and after Lei Jun had married Mr. Ding and joined the circle of people that included first lady Soong Mayling, Mr. Liu allegedly wrote a memoire about Lei Jun (hitherto undiscovered).

Su Ming:

Su Ming traveled with Mr. Zou's household to Chongqing several weeks before the Japanese Imperial Army reached Wuhan in early June 1938. Lei Jun saw Su Ming once in Chongqing several years later, but lost track of her after that.

Bizha and Tao Lei:

Bizha and Tao Lei both still live in Hong Kong. Bizha has had an illustrious 40-year career as the head of international sales manager for a German bra company. With a character of steel, having been "abandoned three times as a child—by mother, father and step-mother" —Bizha remains kind and doting to her little brother, Tao Lei. At age 75, Bizha still plays tennis every day and can beat most players in her group at the club, even those players who are a decade or two younger than she.

Lei Jun:

Lei Jun's youngest child Angela was born in 1958. By this time, Lei Jun's household in Taipei had become the gathering place for members of both extended families. She was a superb cook, and with the help of her sister, Lei Zhao, who lived with them for 30 years, the two sisters nightly fed members from both sides of Lei Jun's family. By the time Angela was born, Lei Jun's immediate family also included Angela's two older brothers, Richard born 1954 and Roland born 1956. When she was not in charge of the kitchen, Lei Jun was most likely playing mahjong. With the generous support of her husband, who had a good paying job along with government perquisites, such as chauffer and security services, Lei Jun cultivated a combination of warmth, humor, generosity, and good will. By 1966, she was able to connect with her first two children, Bizha and Tao Lei. She reunited with them finally when they agreed to fly to Taipei from Hong Kong. The only person in her family of origin who had not made his way to Taiwan was Lei Jun's oldest brother, Yongfeng. The family lost track of his whereabouts in 1953. At age 103, in February 2020, Lei Jun is still living in Taipei City and playing mahjong several times a week. Despite her active social life and the support, she receives from family members around her, Lei Jun still expresses on most days that life for her has been extremely difficult.